Big Southern Hair and Highlights is a heartwarming story that every girl will want to read. Thauwald takes you into the lives of twin sisters (that did not know they were twins) from rural Texas and New Mexico. Readers will have a hard time putting this book down once you have cracked its cover. You will be drawn into the amazing characters and surprised by twists and turns that the girls go through. Big Southern Hair and Highlights is a fun, lighthearted read—with elements of mystery and intrigue, as well as some good life lessons that all young people can benefit from. You will be cheering for the girls and loving their kooky aunts and hoping that all will work out in the end.

Bill Barrett Vice President,
Sales Scholastic Book Fairs
Lake Mary, Florida

This novel is a cross between Each Little Bird That Sings and Steel Magnolias. Chock full of strong southern women, mystery, romance and the ties that bind us together.

Anne Lee
Vice President for Program Development
Scholastic Book Fairs
Lake Mary, Florida

Marsha has written a very sweet book that is both entertaining and heartwarming. A lovely read for anyone who enjoys a good story with a good twist.

Scarlotte Pancerzewski
Author of Old Dog New Trick
Cleburne, Texas

Big Southern Hair is a wonderful book. It has just the right element of mystery along with a friendship that every girl dreams of, a sister!

Stacy and Payton Porter
Mother and Daughter
Waco, Texas

This is a sweet story about how God can take unexpected bumps in the road of life and work them out for good. We may not always have the answers for why things happen the way they do, but love will prevail in the end...no matter what your hair color!

Becca Bell
Education Specialist
Waco, Texas

Big Southern Hair & Highlights

Big Southern Hair & Highlights

please don't dye without us

Tracy,
I hope you enjoy
Big Southern Hair!
Marsha Thauwald
10-6-15

Marsha Thauwald

Illustrated by Erin Weaver

TATE PUBLISHING
AND ENTERPRISES, LLC

Published by Tate Publishing & Enterprises, LLC
127 E. Trade Center Terrace | Mustang, Oklahoma 73064 USA
1.888.361.9473 | www.tatepublishing.com

Tate Publishing is committed to excellence in the publishing industry. The company reflects the philosophy established by the founders, based on Psalm 68:11,
"The Lord gave the word and great was the company of those who published it."

Published in the United States of America

ISBN: 978-1-68142-924-3
1. Family & Relationships / Siblings
2. Fiction / Family Life
15.03.27

Contents

Dedication

I dedicate *Big Southern Hair & Highlights* to my husband, Pete who helped me edit along the way and patiently listened as I described what I wanted the next chapter to be about. I would also like to dedicate this story to my mom, the best role model and encourager a daughter could have.

Acknowledgements

So many people helped me with this writing journey. I would like to thank my daughter, Ashley and granddaughters, Emma and Bethany for their elaborations to *Big Southern Hair & Highlights*. A very special thank you to my editor, Michael Phillips who began the journey with me before I even put pen to paper.

Thanks to Erin Weaver, a talented illustrator who really made *Big Southern Hair* come alive and to a former student, Michael Morrill who was the inspiration for Brother Mike's character.

Heartfelt appreciation goes to Aileen and Kaylyn with The Marfan Foundation for helping me to understand more about Marfan syndrome.

Special acknowledgements to the following people who read the book and let me know what they liked and what I could improve: Pete Thauwald, Chelsea Thauwald, Becca Bell, Stacy and Payton Porter, Leslie and Kimberlyn Smith, Bill Barrett, Anne Lee, Scarlette Pancerzewski, and Donalyn Miller.

I could never have completed the book without any of you and I hope you want to continue the journey with the second book that I have already started writing in my head.

CJ and the Graveyard

Let everything you say be good and helpful so that your
words will be an encouragement to those who hear them.

—Ephesians 4:29 (NIV)

My name is Cora Jean Trinity, but my family and friends
call me CJ. Mama said that my name is special, not
only because I was named after my great aunt Lottie Jean, but
because when she saw me for the very first time, she knew I
was the "core" of her existence. As a teenager, my mom saw
her core as friends, school, and boys. Once she knew I was
coming though, I became her core, and that's how I got my
name. Pretty encouraging for a little girl to hear these words
from her mom, huh? Unfortunately, my mom died right after

I was born, so I had to hear the story of how I got my name from my aunt Lottie, who took me in so I could have "a proper raising from kinfolk." I love my aunt Lottie. She has been a great mother to me. She makes me earn things rather than just giving me what I want. Sometimes I would rather get what I want right away. However, Aunt Lottie says having to earn something and wait for it is building my character. That's why I was surprised when she gave me the diary I am writing in. I didn't even ask for it, but she gave it to me anyway. That means, giving it to me must be special to her, so it's A-OK with me too.

Since Aunt Lottie gave me this diary, I plan to write about the important events in my life. The following experiences are true and not exaggerated—cross my heart.

"CJ, where are you?" hollered Sheriff Tate.

"I'm here! I'm here in a grave in the cemetery!"

I heard footsteps through the ground as he approached, and when I looked up, Sheriff Tate loomed over the grave edge and wondered down at me with big eyes. "Cora Jean Trinity, what on earth are you doing in Mr. Cole's grave?"

"I'm not on earth, Sheriff Tate, I'm in the earth! I fell into this grave when I was looking for a place to get out of the storm."

"Well, lucky for you, this here grave was dug! Mr. Cole's funeral is tomorrow, if I'm not mistaken."

"Thank you, Mr. Cole! Thank you, Sheriff Tate! And thank you, God, for saving me from sure death!" I exclaimed.

As Sheriff Tate figured out a way to get me out of the grave, I counted the blessings in my life. Near death will do that to you. I started thinking about our town, Truway, and all the people who live here. I was born in Truway and have lived here my whole life. This being such a small town, I know just about everything there is to know about the Truway folks and all the exciting things that have happened here.

If you drive north on Texas Road 406 in Buford County toward Del Rio or south toward Piedras Negras, Mexico, you will definitely drive through Truway, Texas, population 402. It's going to be 404 when the 1970 census comes around since the Johnson twins were born in April of 1966. A new birth causes a stir in a small town and two new births, whew, let me tell you, Mr. Johnson was so excited about Mrs. Johnson birthing twins he decided to run a two-for-one special on everything in their store, the Truway General. Across the street at Della's Diner, Della celebrated their births by offering a scoop of vanilla ice cream for anyone who bought the lunch special. The owner of Meryl's Garage advertised a free tune-up to the first person who bought a set of tires for their car. Even Aunt Lottie got caught up in the excitement by offering a free manicure to all customers buying a perm for their hair at the Big Southern Hair Beauty Salon.

Everyone in town turned out for the twins' christening at the nondenominational church at the tail end of Main Street.

We still don't have an ordained preacher, but that's okay with us because we have Brother Mike to lead us in both song and worship every Sunday. If you visit any place in Truway on a Sunday morning, you will hear the people in church, singing at the top of their lungs. Not one of us can carry a tune worth listening to, but when we all sing together, I know God is smiling up there in heaven, surrounded by my mama and all the other angels he has, watching over us.

The folks in Truway love to sing, worship, and celebrate life. My favorite celebration each year is the Chilacothe Farm Summer Festival. The Chilacothes are the most prestigious people in Buford County, or at least the ones with the most money. Aunt Lottie says their farm has been in their family for five generations and has prospered since the third decided to add a thyme garden to the farm. Their specialty is shipping vegetables and fresh thyme to stores nationwide with recipes that explain how adding thyme will enhance the flavor of vegetable dishes. Yellow squash with thyme and pine nuts is the most scrumptious recipe the farm promotes. Of course, their sign at the front entrance of the farm says, "Chilacothe Farms—Where Thyme Makes a Difference!"

I entered a slogan contest sponsored by the Chilacothe Farm Festival Committee the year the Johnson twins were born, the year I turned ten. Since I was starting my life in double digits, which just so happened to be in the double-digit year '66, it was only right that I spread my wings like red-tailed hawks do before they swoop down to pick up their dinner. I decided to swoop in and try my hand at writing something outside of school. Besides, the first prize was the name of the winner added to their slogan used in advertisements in the newspaper, on the radio, and maybe even on television! I may not have won, but I did get third place—a prize of $5 and a framed copy of my slogan. Aunt Lottie was so excited that she hung my slogan in the Big Southern Hair Beauty Salon for all of her customers to see: "Thyme and Thyme Again, Enjoy Chilacothe Farm Foods! by Cora Jean Trinity."

Before I decided to enter the contest that year, my life had been pretty uneventful. Other than hanging out at my aunt's beauty salon, going to school, riding my bicycle around town, and attending church every Sunday, I had nothing else to do. But then the day after I placed in the Chilacothe Farms slogan contest, Aunt Lottie decided that maybe I was old enough to stay home by myself for the rest of the summer. Our house was only half a mile from the Big Southern Hair Beauty Salon. She posted my chores on the refrigerator each morning before she left. I could stay home by myself, so long as I helped out with whatever needed doing.

Today my chores included ironing for our neighbor Mrs. Avery, who could be doing it for herself but decided she was too important to stoop to it. Mrs. Avery and my aunt lived as neighbors since the Great Depression began, and Aunt Lottie wanted to help Mrs. Avery out since she was a widow living alone. Of course, Mrs. Avery was too proud to accept the help, so they worked out a deal. Mrs. Avery paid my aunt $1 per shirt, and I would get fifty cents because I was the one doing the labor. Her half helped with my room and board, or at least that's what Aunt Lottie said. She told me that if I was old enough to stay home, I should oblige myself to help around the house. "With privilege comes responsibility," she warned.

On this particular day, it was too darn hot to iron. I needed a break before finishing my chores, so I went outside. It was so hot I could see the heat waves moving at the end of the driveway. There wasn't a breeze blowing anywhere. If I was going to find one at all, it would have to be on my bicycle. Although Aunt Lottie was okay with me riding my bicycle around town, I rode my bicycle outside of town too. After all, a person can't get the wind blowing in her face just traveling a half mile. No, it would take miles of pedaling as fast I could to feel a breeze. I moved lickety-split past the stores and houses in town and made my way past the city limit's sign. The ride was wonderful!

Several minutes passed before I realized I was riding by the Mount Hope Cemetery where all the Truway folks who have left this earth rest, about five miles away from town. I had never gone so far before on my bike. I began turning around when I felt overcome with a sense of peace as I listened to the birds singing their songs. I smiled with the wind kissing my face. Then nothing. I heard nothing! The birds weren't singing, and the wind wasn't blowing even though I was still moving. The sky was not only getting darker, it seemed to have a greenish hue.

For a moment, time stopped. In that same instance, I heard a roar like a runaway train moving at breakneck speed. The wind picked up and blew so hard I almost fell off my bike. "What is happening?" I asked as the rain pelted my face. Surely, this couldn't be a twister, not in the summertime. I tried to start back to town, but I couldn't see where I was going. The road was gone as if a giant vacuum cleaner had sucked it up and endeavored now to take me along.

The only hope I had of not being lifted into the sky was to throw down my bicycle and try to run for cover. I hurdled the fence beside the road and ran as fast I could into the graveyard. There weren't any buildings, but that would be the biggest blessing in my ten years of life! Instead, I happened upon a grave that had been dug for some poor soul who was leaving this earth. I fell forward and spilled into the grave just as the biggest twister Buford County had ever recorded hit Mount Hope Cemetery. I was literally saved by the grave! Hallelujah!

Of course, when the twister was over, I couldn't figure out how to get out of the six-foot grave. I decided the only thing to do was sit down, sing some of my favorite hymns, and wait for someone to come along to pay their respects or to check out the damage to the grave markers. It was near sunset before I heard Sheriff Tate calling my name as I was singing "Amazing Grace," my favorite hymn of all time.

"CJ! CJ!" Sheriff Tate interrupted my reflections. "You know, CJ, Mrs. Avery found your bicycle parked up in the branches of one of her peach trees." He went on to tell me that Mrs. Avery said she had seen me ride by, headed out of town earlier in the day when I had ironing to do. Now how did she know I had ironing to do at that particular time and not bicycle riding? Everybody always seems to know everyone else's business.

When Sheriff Tate finally got me back to the Big Southern Hair Beauty Salon, my aunt Lottie yelled at me with her eyes all bugged out and her face as red as a pomegranate then she stopped yelling and hugged me close. She was so glad I hadn't blown up into Mrs. Avery's tree along with my bicycle! Even though she was spitting fire mad at me, she cried and let me know she loved me more than anyone else she knew.

That was the last day I got to stay by myself at home. My aunt Lottie decided she would let me do my ironing at the beauty salon along with some other chores she assigned to me. The first of which was to sweep all the dust the twister blew in out of the salon. That particular chore took me three days to complete. We didn't see another twister like the one in '66 until four years later when a new decade started and a series of many firsts began.

Cara and Sam

Trust in the Lord with all your heart and lean not
on your own understanding; in all ways acknowledge
him and he will make your paths straight.

—Proverbs 3:5–6 (NIV)

My name is Cara Louise Tune. I live on the Las Bonitas Ranch outside Whistle Stop, New Mexico, with my aunt Thelma and my constant companion, Sam, the white burro. I am blessed to live on such a beautiful ranch and spend my time with Sam. Many wonderful things have happened to me while living on the ranch, but one of the greatest is having the opportunity to see without my coke-bottled glasses. I have recorded this exciting event in my life, as well as many

Marsha Thauwald

others, in my own personal journal given to me by my aunt Thelma, owner of the Las Bonitas Ranch and my caregiver.

"Cara! Cara Louise Tune, where are you? It's time for us to go!" shouted Aunt Thelma Louise. "Lord, a mercy, girl, don't you know how important being on time to Dr. Grant's office is?"

"I understand! Today is important, Aunt Thelma, but I can't go without telling Sam bye, and he's nowhere in sight!" Sam, my constant companion, is a white burro and has walked beside me around the Las Bonitas Ranch since I was two years old. He is my second shadow. Sam has been such a blessing for a girl who has extreme nearsightedness because of a disease called Marfan syndrome. I also have very long fingers, a curved spine, and loose joints. When I want to, I can bend my thumb backward. Aunt Thelma says that I'm lucky the echocardiogram that I had last year shows my heart and blood vessels are doing okay. However, my nearsightedness is so bad, I am almost legally blind.

When I was four, Dr. Grant sent me to Albuquerque to see medical experts—a geneticist, a cardiologist, and an ophthalmologist—to confirm his suspicions. After days of tests, an echocardiogram, an eye examination called a slit lamp evaluation, and an x-ray that found my back problem confirmed Dr. Grant's prognosis. I don't worry much about

24

all my symptoms. All I want is a normal life like any other twelve-year-old girl.

Without Sam, I wouldn't have all the adventures I have on the ranch. Sam has been my savior on many occasions. He has blocked my path to keep me from stepping on rattlesnakes more times than I can count. I will never forget the first time he kept me from sheer doom. We were walking to the barn to put him in his stall for the evening when I heard this buzzing sound. As I tried to move closer to see, I ran into Sam. He pushed me backward, and I lost my balance and fell. I was mad, but I knew Sam well enough. If he was moving me toward the house, he had his reasons.

When I stood back up, I asked him, "Sam, why did you push me down? What was that sound I heard?" Of course, Sam could not answer my questions, but he turned his head and looked back at the entrance to the barn, and that's when I heard it again, the sound. I knew what it was. It was a rattlesnake! Sam kept the snake from striking either one of us due to his quick reaction to avoid danger. Living in the Southwest on a ranch does sometimes have its challenges, but with Sam around, I am a lot braver than I would be on my own.

The most memorable episode where Sam, the burro, saved me was when I was ten and soaring through the air on an old rope swing. The ranch workers' kids and I were taking turns, swinging across a dried up creek. I felt like a bird flying through the air until the rope broke away from the tree limb it was tied to, and I dropped to the ground with a thud. I landed on a bed of cacti, which broke my fall but didn't keep me from getting the wind knocked out of me. As I lay there, struggling to breathe, I looked up and saw a shadow, blocking the sun. It was Sam. He came to rescue me. I wrapped my arms around his neck and pulled myself up on his back with my face hanging beside his. It was a mile or so to the house, but Sam carried me home, to the back door, without stopping. I hollered for Aunt Thelma, and she brought me in to clean my cuts. She also pulled every cactus sticker from my behind for the rest of the day. Sam stood beside the back door until it got dark. Before I turned in for the night, I went outside and hugged his neck and told him I was okay. I truly love Sam, my seeing-eye burro!

Since Sam could not be found and time was running out, I had to get in the car with Aunt Thelma and go to town to see Dr. Grant. I was excited about a new procedure that might enable me to see without wearing my glasses. I wear glasses to help me see close up; they're so thick people call them coke-bottle glasses, and they magnify my eyes three times their normal size, so when I wear them, I have monster eyes.

Afterward, we get to eat lunch at the Whistle Stop Cafe. I can hardly wait for my favorite lunch—tacos and a big chocolate shake! No place makes better chocolate shakes than the Whistle Stop Cafe! Aunt Thelma told me she remembers ordering chocolate shakes at the grand opening of the Whistle Stop Cafe when she was my age back in 1928. She said the folks in Whistle Stop loved the cafe from day one, so it continued to run through the depression and is thriving still today in 1968. It has a special meaning to me not only because of the chocolate shakes, but because my daddy worked there when he was a young man. The fiftieth anniversary celebration takes place in ten years. I hope I will still be in town.

The drive to the clinic didn't take long at all. We made it to Dr. Grant's office right on time. As soon as the receptionist, Rosalee, checked us in, Dr. Grant met us at the front. We didn't even have to wait in the waiting area. He bent down and looked at me real close and said, "Cara, how would you like to explore the possibility of seeing everything in your life up close and far away without your glasses?"

Of course I answered him by asking, "When can we start?"

"We can start by talking about a brand-new discovery and see how it can help you with your eyesight." He went on to describe how there has been a new research conducted at a place called Cambridge in England that allows doctors to replace clouded lenses with artificial lenses. As a result of the Marfan syndrome, the lenses in my eyes have moved out of place. Dr. Grant says the medical term for this problem is *ectopia lentis* and occurs in more than half the people who have Marfan syndrome. I don't care much for the name. I just want to see better!

The artificial lens should help me see so I can read better. No more coke-bottled glasses. I can't believe it! I want Dr. Grant to schedule the surgery for tomorrow, but he says we have to notify the doctor who studied under the inventor of the lens first. He practices in Hope, Colorado, just outside Denver. Dr. Grant said he already thinks I will be a good candidate for the surgery. Since I am twelve, nearly thirteen, it is a good time to plan a trip to Colorado; however, I will have to wait even longer so that I am at the appropriate age for the surgery. I will be patient so that we can begin the being-able-to-see-better exploration for Cara Louise Tune.

After we stopped for the best lunch ever at the Whistle Stop Cafe, Aunt Thelma ordered her usual chicken tortilla soup with a side salad, and I got my shake and tacos. "How do you feel about everything we learned at Dr. Grant's office today, Cara?" my aunt inquired.

"It's very exciting." Even though according to Dr. Grant, I didn't get Marfan syndrome from either of my parents, I thought about both of them and how I wish they were here now to go through all of this with us. I am one of the 25 percent of people born with Marfan syndrome who did not get it from either my mother or father.

Mom died right after I was born, and Dad was run over by a train late one night behind the Whistle Stop Cafe while walking home. Folks in town said he got his foot hung in the tracks and could not get out of his shoe fast enough to avoid the train. I shudder every time I think about my dad and that night. No one has ever told me details of my mom's death. All I know is, she died right after I was born, and she named me Cara because it means "cherished or beloved one."

As if Aunt Thelma knew what I was thinking about, she said, "You know I wish your parents were here too, but I hope you realize I will be with you for many more lunches at the café!" She stood up from our booth and scooped up her purse from her seat.

She looked at me for a moment and then caught my face between her hands and said as she took her napkin and wiped my mouth, "I love you, Cara Louise, even with your chocolate mustache," We will have the opportunity to talk more about your wonderful new adventure, but now, we need to head on home. Just know that I consider myself very fortunate to care for my namesake."

I smiled and got up to follow my aunt out the door.

When we pulled into the Las Bonitas Ranch, I heard Aunt Thelma say as she squinted against the evening sun, "Something is lying at the edge of the road. It looks like Sam. Oh my gosh, it is Sam!"

I screamed for Aunt Thelma to stop the car. I opened the door and jumped out while it was still moving. Sam raised his head when I called his name, but I could tell he was having a difficult time breathing. Aunt Thelma got out of the car and walked over to inspect Sam's condition. "It looks like a rattlesnake might have bitten him. His leg is swollen, and I don't know what could have caused it to swell like that."

Aunt Thelma said we would have to get the ranch foreman to bring his truck so we could get him to the vet in town. I begged her to let me stay with him while she went to find Juan and his truck. I just kept telling Sam that he would be okay. We would get him help in no time, and he would be back on his feet before supper. I certainly hoped so, but knowing he had lain in the pasture for quite some time, I was not sure he'd be able to pull through.

CJ and the Pink Ladies Club

We can rejoice, too, when we run into problems and trials, for we know that they help us develop endurance.

—Romans 5:3 (NIV)

It's the beginning of a new decade! I don't remember much the last time that happened in 1960. I was just turning four, so I don't remember much. This year I am turning fourteen. What a difference ten years makes! I can't wait to see what happens as I go from fourteen to twenty-four. Can you believe it? In ten years at the start of another new decade, I will be twenty-four—a grown woman. I think I will just be thankful that I am turning fourteen and not rush the rest of this decade.

Now that school has started, I don't have time to ride my bike much anymore. Between my schoolwork and my responsibilities at the Big Southern Hair Beauty Salon, I barely have enough time to write in my diary. My English teacher, Miss Billye Inez Landers, gives us thirty minutes at the end of every day to either read or write independently. Most of the time, I write what has happened at school that day, but sometimes I write about my life outside of school. That's what I want to do today because what happened last Saturday is surely weighing on my mind.

It is my job to pour all the different hair colors from quart containers into applicator bottles and label them so the beauty operators know what color is what at the salon. I take time to complete this job every Saturday morning. We are only open until noon on Saturdays, and on this particular Saturday, there is a line around the block. The ladies' auxiliary luncheon is today, and most of the women in town are going.

Two of our weekly shampoo-and-set customers began talking to each other about a certain "smitten fellow" while under the dryer. They both thought they were being quiet with their discussion, but too bad for those ladies because not only are they hard of hearing, they are under dryers for Pete's sake, driers as loud as parishioners from Brother Mike's Sunday morning sermon. I had just stopped my hair color pouring to move closer so I could hear what they were saying when my detective work was interrupted.

"CJ! Where is the lucky copper hair color I asked you to pour?"

"I put it on the counter in the back room, Aunt Lottie, like you told me to do."

"That's right. I forgot. My memory is starting to fade. Please go get it for me."

Aunt Lottie is not a spring chicken anymore, but she certainly isn't old. Last summer in June, she turned fifty-four. She turned forty when I was born in October of 1956, so it's easy for me to keep up with her age. I just have to add forty to the age I am turning.

Aunt Lottie never married, but I have heard some of the ladies under the dryer talk whenever they don't know I'm listening, and there seems to be a man in Truway who was smitten with my aunt back in the day. I looked up the word *smitten*, and one of its meanings is, "head over heels in love." The ladies under the dryer never gave up the name of that smitten man, but one day, I will find out more. Every girl likes a good romance story!

I finished pouring hair color from one bottle to the next and fetched Aunt Lottie's lucky copper. I had just started in on another job of mine, sweeping up the hair on the floor, when I heard my aunt, screaming, "Oh, my! I don't understand what happened. I know that I put lucky copper on your hair, Gertrude."

I turned around to see what all the commotion was about and saw that Gertrude Jones's hair was a hot pink bubble gum color, not lucky copper! She looked like she wrapped her head in cotton candy rather than having the color of hair she usually has.

Gertrude could not speak as she stared at herself in the mirror. I watched her face as tears streamed down her cheeks. She sat in her chair and cried, then that crying turned to anger. "Lottie Jean Trinity, I have come to this beauty salon for over thirty years, and I have never left it without my lucky copper hair. I have to play the organ for the ladies' auxiliary luncheon this afternoon, and I just can't play that organ with pink hair!" She ripped her apron off, jumped out of the chair, and ran to the bathroom at the back of the salon.

Aunt Lottie slowly turned her head, and our eyes locked. I knew, without a doubt, that I was in big trouble. "Cora Jean, why does this bottle say 'Lucky Copper' when it obviously is *not*?"

I wanted to answer Aunt Lottie right away, but for the life of me, I couldn't figure out what I did wrong. The quart containers we buy come clearly marked. How could there be some strange color in the applicator bottle?

I ran to the closet in the back where I pour the colors from one container to another and took a good look. The one I finished with was lucky copper, one of our most requested hair colors. The label on the container read "Peroxide." Peroxide! No, it's not possible!

Someone was framing me. That's it. Someone was framing me. Someone else must have it in for either me or Gertrude Jones, because I did not put that container of peroxide on this counter! I tried to remember all the faces from the salon, but it seemed everyone in town gathered here this morning.

My investigation came to a halt when I heard more shouts from some of the other ladies in the salon. I ran back to see not one, but three ladies with hot-pink-bubble-gum cotton-candy hair! I filled all the application bottles with Peroxide! Everyone in the room was either crying, shouting, or leaving the premises.

What a day! Aunt Lottie and her other three beauty operators couldn't fix all of their customers' hair in time for the ladies' auxiliary luncheon, so they decided to attend anyway with their new pink hair stuck up under hats that covered their heads. When they had their picture taken due to their service to the community, I wondered if Aunt Lottie was going to hang that picture in the salon as a keepsake? Probably not.

Aunt Lottie didn't talk to me until the next day. She had to open up the beauty salon on Sunday and fix all four of the ladies' pink hair. After that day, I lost my privilege of filling the applicator bottles. Instead, Aunt Lottie made me take one day a week to iron clothes for all the pink ladies who went through the dying process, not once, but twice in twenty-four hours.

A person would think that Aunt Lottie would want to pretend the day of the "Pink Ladies" hadn't happened, but no, instead she had Brother Mike make arrangements with his sign company to add "And Highlights—Please Don't Dye Without Us" on the shop's front window. Aunt Lottie sure does have a sense of humor. I'll say that much for her.

So far, 1970 was the year of one of the biggest catastrophes in Truway, or at least one of the biggest upsets in my life.

We are fixing to have our annual fall festival at school, which is a smaller, but that doesn't mean lesser, version of the Chilacothe Fall Festival. The Chilacothe Summer Festival became the Fall Festival in 1968 because Mrs. Chilacothe complained that being out in the heat of the summer to watch all the festivities was unbearable. So of course, Mr. Chilacothe changed the festival to take place in the fall.

I have entered the sack race and the three-legged race because they are two of my favorite races of all time. I have fast feet, so I got lots of requests to be a partner in the three-legged race. I wrote down all the people's names in my class and pondered the likelihood of them being tied to one of my legs as we finish the race. I still don't care much for boys because they are so unlike girls. They make noises with their bodies and forget to take baths sometimes, and they think it is funny to scare girls with snakes and bugs.

That narrows the list down to girls. I've been thinking seriously about one of the girls who belongs to the only tenant farming family left in Buford County. Her name is Emma Lou. She only comes to school at certain times of the year because she has to work with her family in the fields. She isn't in school right now, but I am going to ride my bicycle over to her house on Chilacothe Farm and ask her about being my three-legged race partner. Besides being fast in races, Emma Lou has a nice smile!

As I was riding and got closer to the farm, I noticed there was a lot of corn in the fields. "So that's why Emma brings so much corn to lunch," I whispered to myself as I peddled as fast as my legs would move. When I started up the driveway, there was Emma Lou, standing by the door, waiting for me with her big smile.

"Howdy, CJ. My ma and pa are shucking corn, so let's cut through the big house and have some milk at my house," suggested Emma Lou.

"Wow! This is beautiful," I marveled, as we walked into the mansion.

"Thanks, but it's not our house. It's Mr. and Mrs. Chilacothe's," Emma Lou explained.

It was the first time I ever saw Emma Lou without a smile on her face. She told me she was doing her chores for Mrs. Chilacothe. That's why I saw her waiting for me. I told Emma Lou about the race at school and made sure I didn't touch anything as we walked through the Chilacothe's house. As we stepped off the back porch, there, a hundred yards ahead, was a much smaller house.

Emma's house was really small, probably not more than two or three rooms. We went through the front door, and to the left was a kitchen area. Emma showed me where she and her little sister, Bea, slept in small beds to the right of the kitchen. There wasn't any living room furniture. I guess they spent their family time in the kitchen, sitting at the table.

Her mama and daddy had a small room of their own. The bathroom was beside their room. I didn't see a bathtub, only a toilet and a sink, but I didn't want to ask Emma Lou how they took their baths. Emma led me back to the kitchen area, and we sat down at the table just as her mom was coming through the back door, carrying a basket of corn.

"Ma, this is CJ Trinity. She wants me to be her partner in the three-legged race over at the school tomorrow. Can I go, Ma? Can I, please?" begged Emma Lou.

"I don't know," said her ma. "Your pa and I need your help putting the shucked corn into baskets for the farm festival this weekend. I'll ask your pa and see if we can spare you for just a little while so you can spend time with CJ in the race."

Emma Lou and I waited in anticipation for her pa's answer. And what do you know, he said she could. That's why I am back at their house early the next morning to fetch her for the annual three-legged race at Kate Willson Elementary School!

"Let's get going. We don't want to be late," I told Emma Lou.

"As soon as I find my tennis shoes, we can go." Emma went to go get her shoes, but when she came back, she did not look happy. "Bea took my tennis shoes. I'm going to have to wear my boots!"

As soon as I heard this, I thought we were doomed until Emma said, "I can go fast in these boots as long as we get us a good rhythm going like one, two, three, one, two, three." She demonstrated, running a few quick paces to prove her point.

"That's fine with me," I said. So I pumped Emma Lou on my handle bars and peddled to Kate Willson Elementary. The line was long, but we made it to the front.

"Oh no! We're going against Bea and her friend, Austin," Emma Lou exclaimed. She leaned over and whispered to me. "You know who Austin is, right?" Austin was Mr. and Mrs. Chilacothe's grandson. His father, Jas Luke, brought Emma's sister and Austin to school. I sure did know him. He started school the year after I did. Even though I said earlier that I don't much care for boys, that Austin sure does have a handsome enough face to make me change my mind.

It looked like it might be a hard competition against Bea and Austin. Ms. Landers was the starter, so she blew her whistle, and the race began. Bea and Austin took the lead. But something must have gone wrong because the next thing I knew they were laying in a big puddle of mud courtesy of last night's rain. We passed them and gained the lead. Keeping that "one, two, three, one, two, three" rhythm really worked because we were the first to cross the finish line! We won the race! Instead of being upset, Bea gave Emma Lou a big hug and looked at me and said, "Congratulations!" Austin looked at me and smiled. He's even more handsome when he smiles.

Emma Lou and I gave each other a high five. I had made a new lifelong friend.

Mrs. Landers gave me special permission to take Emma Lou to my house for a big bowl of ice cream before taking her home. I had just dropped her off in front of the big Chilacothe house when the wind started blowing something fierce. I decided that I better get home quick. I sure didn't want to get caught in another tornado like I did when I was ten.

I barely made it home when I realized that I had to get to the storm cellar! Another twister threatened Truway, Texas. Just as I closed the door and lit the kerosene lamp Aunt Lottie kept in the cellar, I could tell that I got there just in the nick of time by the way the wind started howling. I sat down on the cot to wait out the storm and looked around to make sure there weren't any scorpions. As I peered at the wall behind the cot, I noticed that one of the bricks was coming loose. I took both of my hands and pulled on it to see why it was loose. It came out easily. In the crevice where the brick sat was a book and not just any book—a diary! Whose diary could it be, and how long had it been in this cellar? Why did someone hide a diary in the cellar?

The diary cover looked like leather and was stitched on the edges with leather thread. In the center was one of the most beautiful red stones I had ever seen. I tried to open the small hasp lock, but it wouldn't budge, and there wasn't a key. All I could do was wait for Aunt Lottie to come home safe from the storm and ask her who owned this diary.

Cara and Glen

This is my command—be strong and courageous!
Do not be afraid or discouraged. For the Lord
your God is with you wherever you go.

—Joshua 1:9 (NIV)

Aunt Thelma was right. It was a rattlesnake bite, but thank the Lord, the vet doctored Sam back to health. He had to stay with Doc Lynch for awhile, but he was back at the ranch within a few days.

I don't know what I would do without Sam! He has always come to my rescue, but this time, I got to help rescue him. That night, I knelt by my bed and prayed, "Thank you, God, for saving my best friend, Sam, the one and only seeing-eye white burro in New Mexico and probably in the entire world!" Tomorrow will be a great day as we will begin making plans for our trip to Denver, and I know Sam will get better.

It seemed to take forever, but the day has come. We are on our way to Hope, Colorado, by way of Denver. I had been approved for the artificial lens replacement procedure. I only had to wait two years to get the news. I will be turning fourteen this fall, and I plan to share my Colorado adventure with my friends at a great birthday celebration in October after returning to school.

Dr. Grant gave us a going away party at the clinic before we left the ranch. He even let me bring Sam since it was such a beautiful day to have an outside party in the courtyard. In keeping with the festive spirit, Aunt Thelma draped my daddy's blanket, made by the Tesuque Pueblo Indians, on Sam's back. Not only is the Tesuque Pueblo history common in the Santa Fe area, but the Pueblo is where my daddy grew up before moving to Whistle Stop. Actually, he moved to Las Vegas, New Mexico, before making his way to Whistle Stop. As a matter of fact, he got his chef training at the Charlie's Spic & Span restaurant in Las Vegas before he took over cooking for the Whistle Stop Cafe. One day, I hope to visit the Pueblo since it is a part of my ancestry and then make my way to the Spic & Span restaurant. I don't know how good their tacos are, but I hear their burritos are out of this world!

When it was time to leave, I went to talk to Sam who was outside the back door when I went out to look for him. He looked at me and gave a long wailing bray like he knew something was about to change. I hated to leave Sam on the ranch, but Juan promised to take really good care of him. When we drove away from the ranch house, I looked back and saw Sam standing in the driveway. I almost asked Aunt Thelma to turn around and go back home, but the eye surgery was priority now. Sam will be there when I get back.

There are so many emotions welling up in my heart right now. I'm excited, scared, and anxious—all at the same time. By this time next week, I will be able to see better, hopefully without having to wear thick glasses! Of course, that's if everything goes as expected with the lens replacement procedure. The first thing I want to do when they take the bandages off is to go outside, sit under a big oak tree, and read an entire book in one sitting.

"Cara, what are you thinking about?" asked Aunt Thelma.

Instead of sharing all my thoughts, I simply replied, "Oh, I was just wondering if they have tacos and milkshakes in Colorado."

The hospital is in a place called Hope. Interesting name for a town that has one of the greatest hospitals in the world specializing in artificial lens replacements. The original building went up in the late 1940s just after World War II. The eye surgical wing was added in the early 1960s and dedicated as the Hope Ophthalmology Center in 1968. It is so exciting to know that I will be one of the patients who gets to participate in such a great new procedure!

We met with our contact person, Winona Settler, who works with Dr. Drake, the surgeon replacing my original lens. She gave us a tour of the facilities and then took us to the dormitories where we get to stay until I am officially admitted in two days. Aunt Thelma will get to stay too. I do not know what I would do without her support!

I woke up the next morning, feeling the sun shining on my face, and wondered why since my bedroom is on the west side of the house. Then I remembered I was in Colorado, waiting for Eye Lens Replacement Day (ELR Day). The dormitory apartment was quiet. I got up and went to the door of the main room.

"Aunt Thelma, are you there?" I said, almost in a whisper.

"Yes, Cara, I didn't even hear you. I thought you might want to sleep in since we had such a long drive yesterday."

"How can I sleep in? There are so many things I want to know about this hospital and the eye procedure. Don't we have a meeting set up with Dr. Drake and Ms. Settler this morning?"

"Yes, but let's have breakfast in the cafeteria and then go to our presurgical meeting at ten."

"Okay," I replied. "I'll get ready to join you in thirty minutes. Maybe we can check out the hospital ground and look for big trees to read under."

Aunt Thelma and I went down to the cafeteria and picked out our breakfast. I ate everything on my plate and asked for a second helping of the breakfast potatoes. I have always had a thing for breakfast potatoes smothered in ketchup, not as much as tacos, but they come in a close second!

We made our way across the courtyard to the surgical wing for our meeting. Ms. Settler met us in the hallway. "How did you sleep last night?"

"We slept well, thank you, Ms. Settler," I replied.

"Please call me Winona. And the cafeteria breakfast was okay?"

"The breakfast potatoes were spectacular. There's only one thing I like more than breakfast potatoes, and that's tacos."

Winona smiled at me and asked us to follow her down the hall. We turned into an office and saw a man sitting at a desk. "Dr. Drake, this is Cara and her Aunt Thelma," Winona said.

I liked him right away. "We finally get to meet, Cara. I am so glad you are here. Welcome!" Dr. Drake smiled. He asked if I had any questions, and I told him I wanted to know what his plans were for day after tomorrow.

He laughed and said, "Well, Cara, I will be replacing your eyes' lens with artificial lens. I just completed this same surgery on a young man about your age, maybe a little older. His name is Glen, and he said he would love to talk with you about the surgery and answer any questions. He too has had extreme nearsightedness since he was two years old."

"That's how old I was when I met Sam!" I exclaimed.

"Who is Sam?"

"He happens to be the best snow white burro in the whole world who has been my constant companion at the ranch! I would have had many catastrophes if it wasn't for Sam."

"Well, maybe I can meet him someday."

I told Dr. Drake that I wouldn't mind meeting Glen so all of us went to a room down the hall. As soon as I heard Glen's voice, I knew I liked him.

"Hello there, Cara! How are you?" Glen asked.

"I'm doing okay," I told him.

"Ah, come on, Cara. How are you really doing?"

"I'm doing great *and* hope to be as happy as you seem to be in three or four days!"

"Ask me anything. What do you want to know first?" Glen asked as he leaned back in his chair.

I took a deep breath and asked, "Did you feel the needle when they gave you the painkiller?

"You know, I don't remember feeling any pain—not with a needle or even after the surgery was over. You won't either, Cara. I promise you. Anything else you want to know?"

"No, not right now. I was just curious about whether I'd feel any pain or not."

We left Glen for the day, but he said he would like to meet again tomorrow to answer any more questions.

I went to bed feeling a sense of peace. Meeting everyone at Hope has been a wonderful blessing to me, especially meeting Glen.

The next day, I spent most of my time with Glen. He told me about his surgery, but he also shared his struggles, as well as his triumphs with Marfan syndrome. Who would have thought I would meet someone like me?

His positive attitude is contagious! For most of my life, I have been focused and worried about my eyesight. Glen not only has dealt with extreme nearsightedness, but he has also had to face the fact that his arms, his legs, and his fingers are much longer than even mine. He said that God has given him strength to say something positive each time he is teased in school about his differences.

Like when one of his classmates snickered and then asked him why his arms were so much longer than other students in their school, Glen replied, "I have the ability to reach items on high shelves without a stepladder. That makes me one of the luckiest people I know!" No matter what happens as a result of my eye surgery, I know that after meeting Glen, I will approach everything in my life differently now!

The prep time for the artificial lens procedure was not as bad as I had anticipated. I am now waiting for the ride to the operating room. Phew! The waiting is the hardest part. I have all the confidence in the world in Dr. Drake and his ability to make this surgery as successful for me as it was for Glen.

The needle looked scary, but I wasn't as scared as I thought since Glen reassured me about no pain. As I was thinking about how glad I would be when the surgery was over, I heard a voice. "Cara! Cara, do you hear me? If you can hear me, grab my hand."

I gripped with all my might, not really knowing at this point whose hand I was holding. I feel like I need to climb out of this well to hear exactly who is talking to me.

"Hi, Cara! I love you so much. You did so well!" I would know that voice anywhere.

"Aunt Thelma, is it over? I guess it knocked me out sooner than I expected. I can't believe I have already been through the surgery." I smiled.

I heard someone open the door and walk into the room. "Well, Cara, you're coming around just in time for us to take you back to your room," said Dr. Drake.

I don't even remember being wheeled back to my room. The next thing I remember is feeling the sunshine on my face again. It is the day after the surgery, and even though the darkness surrounds me, I know the sun is shining brightly, and it's going to be a terrific day!

"Hello, Sunshine. That's a good name for you, don't you think, since the sun is shining so much outside. I believe we need to capture some of that wonderful light on the inside too. You're just the person to do that, Cara!" It was Glen, and he had come to see how I was doing.

"What do you say, can we plan an excursion tomorrow? I will pick you up in the chariot of your choice, and we'll wheel around the premises. How about it?" Glen continued with his questions.

"I'd love to go on an outing!" I said.

"Okay, I'll be here to pick you up by eight," Glen exclaimed.

We had a time. We experienced many sights on our getaway even though I couldn't see. Glen described everything he saw and wanted me to know about. He described the building's architecture and even read the dedication sign carved into a brick by the front doors which read, "May all who read this sign know that this hospital staff is dedicated to making the words crystal clear for all who read them."

When we went to the hospital cafeteria, Glen read the menu items to me, and wouldn't you know it, they had breakfast potatoes again. We sat down and talked about our experiences together, our Marfan syndrome, of course, and also the highlights of our tour of the hospital grounds. He said that before I left to return home, he would take me again so that I could see the sights for myself. I have a feeling that the first trip will be just as memorable as the second—thanks to Glen.

"Well, here goes, Cara. The bandages are coming off *now*! I'm going to hand you a mirror to look into first if that is okay with you. Ready?" asked Dr. Drake.

"I'm ready!"

I grasped the handle of the mirror so tightly I was afraid I might break it off. I took a deep breath, held the mirror in front of me, and at first only saw a blurred version of my face, but then my vision cleared, and I looked at my face! That's right! I *looked* at my face and got to look at the color of my eyes without seeing them through thick glasses! My eyes stared right back at me. The person I was looking at was smiling. I put the mirror down and turned to smile at Dr. Drake. Aunt Thelma, Glen, and Winona were all standing behind Dr. Drake, so I smiled the biggest smile I could at the people who supported me.

I looked up so that I could give my best smile to the one who is with me wherever I go!

My new friends in Hope, Colorado, would be missed for sure, but I was going home and see Sam.

First things first. I asked Glen to wheel me outside to the oak tree that he spotted two days ago. I could read my favorite book, *Anne of Green Gables*. Of course, I didn't read the entire book, but I read all the way up to when Anne leaves home to go to school, and that was enough. I could finish the book on my way home.

Two days later, Aunt Thelma and I headed back to Whistle Stop and the Las Bonitas Ranch. Good-bye, Dr. Drake. So long, Winona. Hasta la vista, Glen! I enjoyed my time with all of you, but now I am going back to my buddy, Sam!

Know that this HOSPITAL is dedicated to making the words Crystal Clear for all who read them

CJ and the Diary

Love never gives up, never loses faith, is always
hopeful, and endures through every circumstance.

—1 Corinthians 13:7 (NIV)

Aunt Lottie came, blowing into the house just a few
minutes after the storm blew itself out. "CJ, are you in
here? CJ, answer me this instant!"

"I'm here, Aunt Lottie, and I'm okay. I was able to get
home and into the storm cellar. How are you? Where did you
hide from the storm?"

"I am fine, now that I know you are okay. We all crowded
together in the Big Southern Hair bathroom with our aprons
over our heads. Not that they would have given us any

protection, but at least we were able to hide. The winds didn't seem to be as bad as the twister in '66, but I did see lots of tree limbs, lying in the streets. Hopefully, there was no major damage to any buildings, or heaven forbid, anyone hurt."

"I'm glad you're safe. There's something I want to show you." I picked up the diary from the kitchen table and stuck it out for Aunt Lottie to see.

"Where did you find this, child?"

"I found it in the storm cellar hidden behind a loose brick in the wall. Is it yours?"

Aunt Lottie sighed and said, "No, CJ, it's not mine. It belonged to your mother. After she died, I couldn't find it with any of her things. I was wondering where it got off to."

"It's locked, and I couldn't find a key. Do you know where the key might be?"

"The only place it might be is in your mom's keepsake box she kept under her bed. Do you know where her box is?"

"You let me go through it when I was little up in the attic. I'll go up there and look for it now." I went up to the attic and looked around my mama's things until I found the box, sitting on the floor behind my mother's high school memories. Looking at the box where she kept all her important things seemed to take on a new meaning to me. Why didn't she put her diary in the box with everything else? Are there comments made in her diary that she didn't want Aunt Lottie or me to see?

I opened the lid and peered inside at her prized possessions. Several birthday and valentine cards were tied with a ribbon, and all her report cards for every year she was in school were there. An old dried up flower was in one corner, and underneath the flower were two pictures. The first one had these words on the back, "Me and Jas Luke at the prom—1954." The writing on the back of the second picture was, "Me and Joe on our wedding day, June 5, 1955."

I was sure that neither picture was in this box when I went through it with Aunt Lottie several years ago. I never saw them in any of our family albums either. Aunt Lottie told me that the pictures of my daddy got lost, but that wasn't true. The second photo is a picture of my mama and daddy right before my eyes! He is slender and extremely tall with straight black hair almost to his shoulders. His smile is mesmerizing. There is so much compassion in his face. He obviously truly loved being next to my mama, and she looked so happy being next to him. I took the photos so that I could ask Aunt Lottie where they came from and continued to look through the box. On a lucky rabbit's foot, I found two keys—a house key, and the other might unlock the diary.

I didn't know what to do first, ask about the pictures or see if the key fit the diary and begin the journey of reading my mama's most treasured thoughts and feelings. I chose to unlock the diary and ask about the pictures later at suppertime, so I put the key in the lock and turned it. It opened!

August 27, 1954

Aunt Thelma is thrilled that I came to live with her and go to college at New Mexico Highlands University in Las Vegas. She gave me this beautiful diary as my "Welcome back to the ranch!" present. I start school tomorrow, and I'm excited because I enrolled in the Native Arts Cultural Program where I hope to learn more about their culture and traditions.

As a child, I alternated my time between Aunt Lottie in Texas and Aunt Thelma in New Mexico. I spent most of my school year in Truway but was privileged to go to Whistle Stop in the summers. I remember spending time riding horses around the Las Bonitas Ranch. My love for Native American art began at the ranch when I was around twelve years old.

One day while riding Old Betsy, she stumbled upon what I thought was a big rock in the ground, but upon getting off and checking out her hoof, I discovered part of a pottery artifact. I dug it out of the ground and took it back to the house to show Aunt Thelma. She took me to her cellar and showed me her own artifact collection. There must have been hundreds of shards. She had most of them labeled as to what they might have been used for, and she let me add my piece to the collection. We had so much fun researching the markings on the pottery and finding out it was part of a pitcher made by the Tesuque Pueblo Indians in the early nineteenth century. I continued to search and found many more Tesuque Pueblo Indian pottery pieces through the years, and that's why I want to find out more about their history. Taking the class at Highlands University is going to be so much fun!

August 28, 1954

I will never forget this day. As I sat in my art class the first week of school, I noticed that there were many students who looked Native American. I hoped I would make many friends and learn about their culture and traditions, as much as I would learn from the classes I was going to attend. As I scanned the room, my eyes locked onto a man as he entered. I could not believe how tall he was. He smiled at me as he took a desk to my right. I tried to avert my eyes so he wouldn't think I was staring.

When the class finished, I looked at my watch and realized that I was going to miss my ride back with Juan, the ranch foreman. He had to be back at the ranch before dusk to feed the cows. This morning, I had told him to go ahead without me, and I would call Aunt Thelma to come into town and have dinner with me. However, going back to the ranch and having dinner in front of the big rock fireplace was more appealing.

As I was running down the steps in front of the Culinary Arts Building, I tripped on a step and felt myself falling. There wasn't anything I could do to avoid a very bad spill. Even though everything happened so fast, I remember thinking about how Aunt Thelma would still have to drive into town and come see me in the hospital with a broken leg or worse. Suddenly, I felt a strong grip on my arm and saw someone standing in front of me. The only thing broken was the heel on my shoe.

I was so thankful for not falling. I wrapped my arms around the neck of the person in front and me and buried my face in his shirt as I murmured, "Thank you so much for saving me. How did you move so quickly?"

"You left your notebook under your desk, and I was chasing after you to give it to you. I couldn't yell out your name, 'cause I didn't know it," he said. "I was right beside you and saw you trip."

The whole time he was talking, I was lost in his beautiful brown eyes. I didn't realize that he was asking me a question until he repeated it. "Hey, I asked your name. You're not in shock or something, are you?"

"No, I'm sorry. I was lost in thought for a moment. My name is Jean. What's yours?"

"Joe. Joe Smallwood." There was nothing small about Joe. He had to be at least 6 foot 5 inches. He had straight, raven hair, high cheek bones, beautiful brown eyes, and the sweetest smile."

This was no time to get interested in a man, no matter how handsome he was! I just had my heart broken in Texas less than six months ago. No, I would

need to keep my distance from Joe. It was not fair to
lead him on when I knew that I needed time to think
about what I wanted for my life.

I stopped reading and took a deep breath. I was actually
reading something my mama wrote with her own hand. She
met my daddy on her first day of class! I wanted to let Aunt
Lottie know that I found the key and was able to read one
of the most memorable times in her life, the day she met the
man she would later marry. "Aunt Lottie! You're never going
to believe it. I found the key to the diary, and I read the very
first entry. My mama wrote about how she met my daddy!
Aunt Lottie, why didn't you tell me you had this picture? You
told me that all the pictures of my daddy were lost."

"Oh, CJ, I'm so sorry. To be honest, I found that picture
of your daddy in your mama's Bible when I was packing away
the rest of her things a few months ago. You were at school,
and I planned to show it to you, so I put both pictures in
the box with the other keepsakes. I wanted to give you her
Bible and the keepsake box, but with so many things to think
about, I forgot. I am sorry. I hope you will forgive me."

"Of course, I forgive you! I just can't believe all of this
is happening. I won the three-legged race with Emma Lou,
I was saved from a storm, I found a mysterious diary that
happens to belong to my mama, and I found a picture of my
mama with my daddy while looking for the key to the diary!
What's going to happen next?"

I shouldn't have asked out loud. So many things happened right after one another and I have been in somewhat of a state of shock for a couple of weeks and am just able to pull my wits together to describe it all at this time.

When Aunt Lottie and I sat down to have supper the night I found the diary, she let me know about something else that was on her very busy mind.

"CJ, how would you like to go to a very prestigious boarding school away from home to prepare you for college?"

"Why would I want to do that? What does *prestigious* mean, anyhow?"

"Well, you and I have talked about you getting into a good college in a few years, and I think it would be a great idea for you to pursue the rest of your education in an award-winning private school. An award-winning school, a prestigious one that could challenge you."

"I don't know, Aunt Lottie. Leaving home right now doesn't feel comfortable to me. How long have you been planning on sending me away?"

"Actually, there is something else you need to know."

There's something else *I need to know? What now?* I thought.

"CJ, you need to sit down on that divan."

Oh, no, Aunt Lottie was using a high society word for "sofa," so that meant she was really serious.

"CJ, I don't know how to start."

"Start from the beginning," I said.

"I can't. That will take longer than we have time for at this moment. I will just tell you the most important part, and then I will fill you in on all the other details later, okay?"

"Aunt Lottie, just *tell* me!"

"Okay, okay. CJ, you have a sister." I stared at Aunt Lottie for what seemed like an eternity before saying anything.

"I have a sister?"

"Yes, you have a sister, and not only is she your sister, she's your twin. You have a twin sister."

"You can't possibly mean what you are saying! If I had a sister, I would have known about her before now. How could you tease me like this?"

"I am not teasing you, CJ! You have a twin sister who lives in New Mexico with my sister, Thelma Louise. They live on a ranch, and I didn't tell you before now because Cara has been unable to see very well until just recently. She could not have the eye surgery until she was older, and that was just this summer, so we decided, Thelma and me, that it would be best if we waited to tell you about each other. We think that the best place for you to be together without sending her here or you there is to enroll you in a school that would prepare you both for your college careers." As I tried to listen to everything Aunt Lottie was saying, all I could think of was that I had a sister whose name resembled mine.

"Her name is Cara? Cara what?"

"Cara Louise Tune. My sister's last name is Tune, so it made sense for her to be Cara Louise Tune. Thelma's husband, Henry, was killed in World War II when his army tank he was driving ran over a land mine in Europe. He left his ranch to Thelma, and that's where she and Cara live, the Las Bonitas Ranch outside Whistle Stop, New Mexico. We thought it would make more sense for Cara to grow up on the ranch since she had special needs that would require many doctors' visits. Besides, I had to work at the salon and really couldn't take care of two little girls. We thought it would be a good idea for each one of us to take care of one of you, so you grew up here in Texas, and Cara grew up in New Mexico."

"How could you have been so selfish? My sister should have been with me growing up and me growing up with her! We could have spent our entire childhood getting to know one another!" I said, exasperated.

"I realize that in hindsight. Maybe we could have done it differently, but we did what we thought was best for both of you at the time. All I can say is, I'm sorry for the mistakes I've made. However, if I listed all of my mistakes in life, you and I would both be very old and I'd be dead before I finished listing them. Please forgive me, CJ. You are going to have to trust me and know that my heart was in the right place at the time, as well as Thelma's. We had just lost your mama, and we both wanted to be a part of your lives. Whether you understand why we made our decision to separate you for a short period of time is not what is important now. What's important is you get to spend time with Cara for many years to come. Do you want to get started or not?" The look on Aunt Lottie's face was one of guilt, but the love for me still shone through.

Many days passed before I could be in the same room with Aunt Lottie. It wasn't as simple as she made it out to be. A person can't just relocate and live with another person they didn't know, even if they happened to be a twin sister. I needed help in coming to terms with my life. After all, folks say your teenage years are the hardest. Maybe this is why. Maybe things happen that we don't know are going to happen, and it's just a lot to take in.

I decided to talk with Brother Mike at the church. He is such an inspiration and someone I highly respect. He has been our interim pastor for several years because we can't seem to find the right pastor to take over. Brother Mike is not ordained to be a preacher, but he is preaching all the same every Sunday unless we have a visiting preacher come through town.

Brother Mike Morris joined our church before I was born. He became the music minister very soon after he joined. Aunt Lottie said you could hear his voice over everyone else's when the hymns were sung, so they thought it was right to have Brother Mike be the music leader.

I went to the church office and found Brother Mike deep in thought, sitting at his desk chair with his crutches propped against the wall. Brother Mike was born with cerebral palsy and could not walk without them. He is admired by all the folks in Truway because of his perseverance to do God's will and help others in his path. I shared my story with him about how I found my mama's diary and how I found out I have a twin sister.

"Brother Mike, how I am supposed to go live the rest of my life with a sister I don't even know in a place I have never been?"

"CJ, I know you have taken on quite a lot in the past few days, but life is full of challenges, especially as we get older. Our challenges are what make us stronger. God never said that we would have only good times. We have to take hold of everything that comes our way and have faith that it is going to be okay."

"I want to believe that too, Brother Mike. That's why I'm here. I just need encouraging that's all. I do want to meet my twin sister and spend time with her. It's just so scary to think about leaving somewhere I feel comfortable and take a journey to the unknown."

"CJ, believe me, I understand. When I was growing up, I had a very difficult time fitting in at school. I wanted to run and play like all the other kids. One night, I was crying and feeling sorry for myself. My mom came into my room and she said, 'Michael, God gives us all different talents. Yours may not be to win races. Your talent is a special talent that God gave you, and even if you don't know what it is right now, you will. He will show you.'

"I believe that I am spending my life now using talents God gave me. My mom died a couple of years ago, but I still hear her. So, CJ, you are on a quest to find your talents. I know one of your talents is encouraging others, so maybe it's time for you to be there for your sister and others you encounter at school."

The talk with Brother Mike is what I needed. I realize how much I respect not only him but all those who have crossed my path. We all face challenges, but God has a plan for us! I just don't know my plan yet!

So many things are running through my mind. My mom kept a diary, which she hid in the cellar, Aunt Lottie was sending me away to school, I have a twin sister, and my daddy was the most handsome man I have ever seen. Time to face the music.

My immediate plan of action was to apologize to Aunt Lottie for my behavior. When I rode my bicycle into our driveway, a strange car was parked in front. *Who could be at our house at this time of day?* I asked myself.

I walked into the house, and my aunt's face looked like someone had died.

"Aunt Lottie, is everything all right?"

"Yes, CJ. We have a visitor. She came to specifically see you. This is Geraldine Chilacothe from the Chilacothe Farms. I believe you know Emma Lou and her family who work for the Chilacothes and maybe her grandson, Austin."

The woman sitting across from my aunt turned, tilted her head to the side, and raised her eyebrows. There was a smile on her face, but I couldn't see the smile in her eyes. They seemed cold.

"Well, hello, CJ! I have been meaning to meet you in person for quite some time now. I saw your name when we were going through the winners of our last poster contest. Congratulations! You are very creative. Your Aunt Lottie told me that you love to write," Mrs. Chilacothe remarked.

As she was talking, I could not help but wonder why she was telling me all of this!

Mrs. Chilacothie continued, "You know your mother loved to write too. As a matter of fact, I know she kept a diary and tried to write in it every day. I don't know if you knew or not, but your mother worked for me for a while before she passed away."

No, I did not know that my mother worked for the Chilacothes, I thought.

"Anyway, I heard that you know about your twin sister and are planning to go away to school with her in El Paso. I was wondering if you have been able to find your mother's diary? We never found it after she left us. The diary would be a great way for you to get to know your mother before you reunite with your sister. So have you found it by chance?" hissed Mrs. Chilacothe.

Something about the way Mrs. Chilacothe was looking at me reminded me of a snake. She even made a hissing sound when she talked. Her presence in our house made me feel like I needed to turn and run, but I knew I couldn't be impolite to a guest. Instead, I looked her straight in the eye and lied, "No, Mrs. Chilacothe, I haven't found my mama's diary. Maybe my sister has it, but it's not here. I will ask her when I see her. You are right. Reading it together would be a wonderful way for Cara and me to get to know our mama and spend time with each other too. Thanks for stopping by and congratulating me and all, but I have homework I need to do for school."

Mrs. Chilacothe's smile left her face very quickly, and the look in her eyes became even colder. She made another hissing sound as she turned and walked toward the front door. I just wish she would slither away. "Lottie, it was so good to visit with you after so many years. We should spend more time together now that CJ will be away from home. Maybe you could come out to the farm for lunch soon."

"I would like to have lunch, Geraldine, but the salon keeps me busy, so I don't see a lunch with you anytime soon. Please tell John Mark that I said hello, and that I hope he is doing well," Aunt Lottie said as she walked toward the door.

At the sound of her husband's name, Mrs. Chilacothe's face turned angry red. She mumbled her good-byes and left in a hurry.

After she was gone, I could still smell her pungent perfume—an overpowering sweet almond smell. It was suffocating!

Why did she seem to be so interested in my mama's diary, and how did she know about going away to school with Cara?

Cara and CJ

And we know that God causes everything to work
together for the good of those who love God and
are called according to his purpose for them.

—Romans 8:28 (NIV)

I read the letter again while I was waiting to meet my sister.
I read it four times already, so I figured one more time
wouldn't hurt.

Dear Cara Louise,

You don't know me yet, but I decided to write you and
introduce myself. My name is Cora, Cora Jean Trinity,
but I go by CJ. I am fourteen years old, and I live in
Truway, Texas.

I have curly strawberry blond hair, hazel eyes, a sprinkling of freckles across my nose, and I am your twin sister.

Aunt Lottie just told me about you two weeks ago. She says that Aunt Thelma, another person I have not met, has also told you about me. I sure would have liked to have seen the look on your face when you found out about me. You probably had the same look on your face that I had when I heard about you!

Can you believe it? We are twins. We have the same birthday, and we spent the first fourteen years of our lives without knowing the other existed. Sometimes I just have to take a deep breath and say out loud, "I have a sister!"

I can hardly wait to meet you in person. I guess we are going to get that chance right after Christmas. It seems strange to be starting the new year in a new school, but knowing that you will be there makes it a little less scary.

There is so much to tell you. I want to wait and tell you more face to face, so I will close for now. See you at the Greensboro School for Girls in El Paso in January!

Your sister,
CJ

I folded the letter and put it back into my bag with my letter from Glen. He and I have been writing each other ever since the day I got home from Hope Hospital. Glen began his junior year in high school and got his driver's license. For some reason, I have not told him about CJ yet. I guess I want to meet her in person first. I did tell him about going to El Paso to complete my high school education in an all girls' school. He said that it was "groovy" to be going to a school away from home, and he looked forward to hearing all about it once I arrived and got settled.

The drive from Whistle Stop was long but not unbearable. I read some but spent most of my time thinking about my sister. CJ said she has curly strawberry blond hair. I wonder if it is long or short. Is she as tall as me? Does she like to read? At least I know we are the same age. I would know the answers to my questions in the next few hours.

As we got closer to El Paso and our destination, I wondered what Greensboro would be like. Even though we were in West Texas where Mesquite trees and cactus are abundant, the Bigtooth Maples that lined the road leading up to the school were majestic. The tree branches were bare since it was winter time, but just imagine what they will look like in the spring! Now they looked like a line of soldiers protecting the road. As soon as CJ and I get our things put away in our dorm room, maybe she will go with me to the school library to find out more about Bigtooth Maples. I found out what kind of trees grow in the area before we left the ranch. Would she want to spend time in a library with me?

When the sign for the Greensboro School for Girls was right in front of me, I knew we had arrived! A woman came out of the administration building and stood on the front steps before our car stopped. She must have been looking for us. Aunt Thelma and I got out and walked up to the massive red brick building. Beautiful sculptured white columns supported the front awning.

The lady standing on the top step, wearing a blue suit and looking very important, said, "Hello, Cara! This must be your Aunt Thelma. My name is Dean Wittingham, and I am thrilled to be the one to welcome you personally to Greensboro."

"Hi, Dean Wittingham. Yes, this is my Aunt Thelma. I know you two have already had great conversations on the phone about my sister and me, huh?"

The dean stared at me for a few seconds and then said, "Well, yes, I do know about your circumstances. Your sister is not here yet. You are the first to arrive. I thought it would be best to take you on the tour of the grounds once she gets here. Meanwhile, I have tea and sugar cookies being sent to our drawing room and thought we could chat and answer any questions you might have. I hope that's okay with you." She then turned and led us into the room where I would finally meet my sister.

While we were walking inside, Dean Wittingham asked me a lot of questions about my hobbies, but I did not tell her much more than the fact that I am an avid reader. I want to save my comments about my life to share with CJ. I feel like I need to pinch myself to make sure I am not in a dream. I can't believe I have a twin sister.

Aunt Thelma asked the dean if there was a place they could visit with each other while I relax. So here I sit, waiting on them to get back, waiting on CJ, and waiting to begin a new adventure.

While they were gone, I looked around at my new surroundings. The drawing room was decorated with elaborate Victorian furniture: a scarlet velvet couch, love seat, and two matching arm chairs. A grand piano graced the back wall behind us. The walls were papered with textured prints of green and gold. There was a silver tray on the coffee table in front of the couch with a teapot and several sugar-coated cookies on a platter. I have never had hot tea before, so I felt all grown now. Of course, I am very familiar with sugar cookies, so I was glad we would start our chat eating a familiar food. The cookies sure were looking good, so in order to keep myself from sampling one before my aunt and the dean returned, I decided to investigate the piano. The closer I got to it, the more grand it became. I sat on the soft velvet cushion and stared at the keys. Would the people from the school mind if I played a tune on this beautiful piano? Since the building seemed pretty quiet, I decided I would give myself permission to play. "Danny Boy" called out to me:

> Oh Danny boy, the pipes, the pipes are calling
> From glen to glen, and down the mountain side
> The summer's gone, and all the roses falling
> 'Tis you, 'tis you must go and I must bide.
> (Frederick Weatherly, 1913)

Aunt Thelma used to sing this song to me when I was little before going to sleep at night. She told me she used to sing it to my mom too. I've always loved music, so she bought us a piano. My long fingers were good for playing, so I tried to play every day after I got home from school. I was glad that I could return here and play songs that would remind me of home, Aunt Thelma, and Sam. I walked back to the couch to rest.

I must have fallen asleep while sitting in the drawing room because I heard someone call my name like in a dream. When I opened my eyes, I didn't see a soul. "Cara, Cara Louise, where are you?"

"I'm here in the drawing room. Who's calling me?"

"Oh, there you are. Can you believe this place? It's like a museum. The woman at the desk in the foyer told me you were in the drawing room, but there are so many rooms to choose from, and none of them labeled The Drawing Room, so I called out to you. Standing before me was the one person I wanted to see more than anyone else in my life.

"Hi, Cara! It's me, CJ. Of course, you probably already figured that out. Hey, I like your hair. It's longer than mine, wouldn't you agree? Stand up so that I can see if we are the same height, okay?"

"CJ, you're here. I can't believe it!" When I stood up to see who was taller, I suddenly reached out and wrapped my arms around CJ's neck, and she wrapped her arms around me. She stepped back and stared at me for a second. Then she smiled at me with the most beautiful smile I had ever seen—a sister's smile.

"Cara, you're a lot taller than me! I guess I thought we would look just alike, but it makes sense that we don't since we are fraternal twins. As soon as we get to our dormitory room, let's measure each other and mark the heights on the bathroom doorframe to commemorate, which means 'to remember' this day of our meeting. What do you say?"

It's funny that the things I wondered about CJ were the exact same things she talked about with me. Her hair is naturally curly and a lot lighter than mine. She has hazel eyes like she said in her letter. I have brown. Just then, Aunt Thelma came back into the drawing room with the dean and another lady who looked like Aunt Thelma.

"Cara, it's so wonderful to see you again. You don't remember me, but I am your aunt Lottie."

"Hello, Aunt Lottie. I have heard a lot about you in the last few weeks. Aunt Thelma, guess who this is standing beside me?"

"How many guesses do I get? CJ, how in the world are you?"

"I'm just peachy now that we are all here standing in the same place. Thank you, Aunt Thelma, for bringing Cara to El Paso." She smiled and squeezed my shoulder.

"You are so welcome. Lottie and I have dreamed about this day for a very long time, right, Lottie?"

"Yes, it has been a very long time, Thelma."

The two older sisters embraced each other and then stood back and stared at each other with tears in their eyes. I turned and smiled at CJ, and she smiled back as we both took in the moment.

Dean Wittingham took us all on a tour of the Greensboro School for Girls. She told us the school was founded in 1937. Only the most wealthy families could afford to send their daughters to Greensboro up until 1954. After that year, the school became a preparatory school for college bound girls in Greensboro whether they were from a wealthy family or not. There was a philanthropist in the area who wanted to give scholarship money to girls who showed academic promise and wanted to attend Greensboro. Each year, his family awarded five scholarships to girls who applied and met their criteria. Since we were accepted to Greensboro without applying, Aunt Thelma and Aunt Lottie either had a secret stash of money somewhere, or they filled out the applications for us. I would need to find out more about how we got here, but not now.

CJ and I were sitting in our room after a two-hour tour and a small lunch of tuna sandwiches and tomato soup in the cafeteria. We were the only ones in the cafeteria; the other students had not returned from their Christmas break yet. We arrived early since we were new, and it was the middle of a school year. Our aunts left us for the rest of the day so that we could unpack and get to know one another. They planned to spend the night in a nearby hotel and then pick us up for breakfast in the morning before they went their separate directions once again.

"Well, I guess this will be our home for the next few years, Cara. These beds seem comfy enough, and I'm so glad that we are in a dorm with bathrooms attached. Some of the dorms have one community bathroom per floor. I wouldn't like to take a shower in a place where others were also taking a shower in the same room, privacy curtains or not. How about you?"

"I like the room too, CJ. Look at the view of the mountains outside our window. Did you notice the benches under the Bigtooth Maple around the school grounds on our tour? We can sit out under the trees and read when the weather gets a little warmer and the maples have leaves."

CJ walked toward the window and peered outside. "Oh, is that what you call those?

"I didn't even think about what kind of trees were around. I don't read a whole lot, but I do like to write. Did you know our mother liked to write too? She kept a diary. I found it hidden behind a brick in our storm cellar. Would you like to read it with me? I only read the first entry. Once I found out about you, I decided to wait and read the rest of it with you."

Our mother kept a diary? I couldn't wait to read her diary and find out more about who she was, what she was like, and if any of her dreams came true for her. "Of course, I want to read it with you, CJ. I can hardly wait to find out more about our mom. Let's get started right away."

She went to her suitcase and pulled out a leather-bound book with a beautiful stone on the cover.

"Okay, Cara, but before we begin, I have to tell you about a visit Aunt Lottie and I had from one of the richest ladies in Truway. Her name is Geraldine Chilacothe, and she was so 'nice' that sugar could have melted in her mouth, except instead of having sugar in her mouth, I think she probably makes her own venom. She is such a snake. She even hisses when she talks and slithers when she walks. I knew she couldn't be trusted the minute I laid eyes on her. She wanted to know if I found mama's diary. I lied, even though we shouldn't be lying, and told her, 'no.' Why do you think she wanted to know about Mama's diary, Cara?"

"That's so strange. It sounds sinister, especially probing you to see if you had Mom's diary. I wonder if we will pick up any clues as to why she's so interested? Did you find any pictures of Mom and Dad by chance?" I asked CJ.

"Yes, let me get the diary and pictures and show you. I like the word *probing*. That's exactly what Mrs. Chilacothe was doing, sticking her nose in a place where it didn't belong," CJ replied as she rummaged through her suitcase. She handed me an envelope containing two pictures.

As I examined the first one, I said, "That is the same picture Aunt Thelma has of Mom and Dad. Isn't she beautiful? Dad was so handsome. They made a great couple. Don't you think you look like Mom, and I favor Dad? Who is with Mom in this other picture?"

"Read what it says on the back. That is Mama's first love, Jas Luke from her high school days, who just happens to be the son of Geraldine Chilacothe," CJ answered.

CJ and I read the first entry about Mom meeting our dad. It was so romantic. Reading the rest of Mom's diary was going to be so much fun!

I could not imagine a day more eventful than this one. I soon found out that this day was only one of many more exciting days to come.

Jean and Joe

And now these three remain: faith, hope and love. But the greatest of these is love.

—1 Corinthians 13:13 (NIV)

December 24, 1954

Joe and I have been inseparable ever since that first day of class. So much for trying to play it cool. The second day in class, our eyes met again, and when he smiled at me and asked if I would have a cola with him after class, I heard myself answering, "I would love that!" The rest of our days have been spent together. Joe told me later that he knew that we would become close friends the moment we met. Between school and spending time with Joe, I haven't taken the time to write.

We are about to spend our first Christmas together at the ranch. He told me that he didn't know if he could wait until tomorrow to give me my present, but I insisted we wait and exchange gifts after a good breakfast and a second cup of Aunt Thelma's famous egg coffee. Supposedly, the egg settles the grounds in the coffee pot so they don't end up at the bottom of your cup. Apparently, it works because I have never found coffee grounds in my cup. While I was thinking about our morning coffee, I noticed Joe was already walking toward the front door, but then he stopped and turned around and said, "Jean, I love you. You know that, don't you?"

As soon as I caught my breath, I responded, "I know. I love you too." I answered him right away with a smile. He continued out the door and got in his old truck and drove away.

December 25, 1954

It's Christmas Day, the Lord's birthday! I got to spend it with two of my favorite people. We ate our breakfast and went to the den for our egg coffee and gift exchange. Joe handed me a small package and grabbed Aunt Thelma by the arm, pulling her closer to me. When I opened the tiny box and peered inside, I could not believe what I was seeing. It was the most spectacular silver ring with turquoise and coral stones in a very unique setting! Before I could find my voice, Joe knelt down and lifted my face up to his and asked, "Jean Louise, will you marry me?"

We talked about getting married someday, but now, while we are in the middle of our studies? I did not know what to say, but then, "Yes, I will marry you, but I want to know more about this ring."

"It was made by my grandfather and given to my grandmother before they were married. It has been passed down to the oldest son so that it can be a symbol of love and commitment for a lifetime together," Joe said. "I only wish my mother and father were around to meet you and see the family ring on your finger."

"What a special story. I feel so honored to be able to wear this family heirloom. I will treasure it always," I exclaimed with tears in my eyes.

This was the first time Joe said anything about his mom and dad. I wanted to know more about where they might be, and I wondered if he had other relatives somewhere in New Mexico, but I knew that Joe would tell me when he was ready.

Aunt Thelma gave us her blessing but said she hoped we would wait awhile before setting a date since we were both in school. She said we had our whole life to spend together. We didn't need to rush into anything yet.

What a day! I can't believe I am going to marry Joe and stay in New Mexico indefinitely. Tomorrow, we are all driving into Las Vegas and eating at Charlie's Spic and Span Mexican Restaurant to celebrate Christmas and our engagement. The burritos at Charlie's are legendary, and I can hardly wait to sink my teeth into one covered with green chili and gobs of cheese inside!

Life is good.

C ara asked me to stop reading for a second. She said, "Mom loved Mexican food as much as I do."

"I didn't know you liked Mexican food. Are burritos your favorite?" I asked.

"I like burritos but not as much as Aunt Thelma. My favorite is tacos with a chocolate shake to go with them."

"Well, that's good to know. Don't you like the part where she described the family ring and what it meant when given to a loved one? That's so romantic."

"I wonder where Mom's ring is. Do you think she was buried with it still on her finger?"

"Maybe we'll find out before we get to the end. Let's go get something to eat before the cafeteria closes. Talking about burritos and tacos has made me hungry," I suggested to Cara.

June 5, 1955

This is the happiest day of my life! I thought I would never love someone like I did Jas Luke, but I was wrong. I love Joe with all my heart, and today is our wedding day. He added a huge coral stone to the front of my diary as my wedding present from him. He took something he knew was special to me and made it even more special.

Joe is such a wonderful man. Not only is he handsome and creative, he is also a great chef. Since Joe is a cook at the Whistle Stop Cafe, I don't think I will have to do much of the cooking in our apartment. He told me that when he prepares meals at the café, he pretends he is making every dish for me, and he brings our supper home almost every night.

I am going to be working at the city hall as a receptionist for the government offices but not before we get a few days to set up our home. We will spend two glorious days at the Plaza Hotel. I have wanted to see inside that hotel for a long time. I am so happy and thank the Lord for my blessings.

"I wish we could have seen Mama and Daddy on their wedding day," I exclaimed.

"Can't you just see the love between them in Mom's words?" I asked. "Let's keep reading to see how they spent their honeymoon."

June 7, 1955

The Plaza Hotel was absolutely amazing! We got the honeymoon suite and ordered room service for breakfast. Joe took me on a tour of Las Vegas, and then we went by Charlie's Spic and Span Mexican

Restaurant. We didn't go inside the restaurant on this trip. We only had the rest of the day before returning to Whistle Stop. He promised that we would go back and stay longer in Las Vegas when he had more vacation days, to see old friends and eat burritos. I think it would be wonderful to spend Christmas at the Plaza and eat at the cafe. Maybe Aunt Thelma would leave the ranch long enough to go with us again. She deserves a vacation anyway. She never leaves the ranch much. I will ask Joe how he feels about the plan when he comes home from work.

My work week at the city hall does not start until next Monday. It would be great to spend time decorating our new home and reading some of my old journal entries that I found in an old notebook. The first one I turned to was one I had written the day after high school graduation, May 24, 1954. Jas Luke broke up with me the night before. He said he had to go away to college, and it would be best if "he wasn't tied down" while he was away at Harvard. He also told me that I shouldn't have to be tied down either for four years. I knew the real reason he was breaking up with me. His mother told him they would not send Jas Luke to the university of his dreams if he continued to see me anymore.

His mother has never liked me. For some reason, she doesn't seem to like Aunt Lottie either. You could tell how she felt about people. Her eyes made you feel cold when she looked at you.

As heartbroken as I was, it was for the best. Aunt Lottie talked me into coming to visit Aunt Thelma and get away for awhile. The rest is history.

I stopped reading for a moment and said to Cara, "I have seen that cold stare in person! Jas Luke's mom is not a very warm person. Aren't you glad that our mama didn't marry him? What a nightmare that would have been—living under the same roof as Geraldine Chilacothe."

"CJ, we wouldn't be the same people if our mom had married Jas Luke. As a matter of fact, we wouldn't exist, so yes, I am glad that our mom married our dad, Let's keep reading. I want to know more about Mom and Dad in the early years," Cara insisted.

June 11, 1955

I started my job at the city hall today. The city manager gave me a tour of the building and went over my responsibilities. It is so exciting that I will get to continue my studies at Highland two days a week and work three days once school kicks off for the fall. Joe decided to take a semester off and concentrate on his job at the cafe. Mr. Ortiz, the owner, is thinking about starting another cafe in a town just south of Whistle Stop, so he plans to leave Joe in charge while he is out of town.

Joe will be making more money which he says I can use for my gas money to and from Las Vegas. He's going to let me drive his truck since he won't need it during the day while he's at work. Between learning a new job and helping Joe at the cafe. This is going to be one fast summer.

August 20, 1955

Well, I was right about one thing—the summer flew by. I have had a wonderful time working with the people in Whistle Stop and seeing them on the weekends at the cafe. I start school tomorrow. It will be sad to go to Highland without Joe, but I am excited about going back to my classes.

I am so tired for some reason. Lately, I have noticed my energy level has diminished. I used to love to go running after work, but now I don't have the strength to walk a mile, much less run three. I think I will make a doctor's appointment soon, but not now. There's too much to do. Joe brought home some vitamins for me to start taking. He thinks that I am doing too much. We will see.

August 22, 1955

I can't believe what has happened in the last twenty-four hours. I will start with my ride to school yesterday morning. I was driving the truck and singing my favorite song, *Danny Boy*, when I heard a loud pop, and the truck swerved.

I was able to keep the truck steady and slowed down to pull off the road. A red sports car passed me as I pulled to the shoulder. The driver turned and gave me a dirty look before passing me. He obviously was in a big hurry. I stopped the truck and got out to investigate what happened. Sure enough, the front tire was flat. I looked up and saw the red sports car coming back toward me. He must not be in that big of a hurry. When he saw the situation, he asked me if I had a spare tire.

We found it in the bed of the truck, but when I thought he was going to offer to change the tire, he said he would rather take me into town and hire someone to come out and change it instead.

My instincts were to decline his offer, wait for him to drive away, and then start walking back to a farmhouse I saw a few miles back so that I could call Joe to come get me. When I told him no thanks, I would take care of the flat, he grabbed my arm and sneered at me, saying I shouldn't get so uppity. I heard a siren go off behind me and a voice coming from a bullhorn, "Take your hands off the lady's arm and step back."

The sheriff from Whistle Stop was on his way to Las Vegas and noticed Joe's truck and realized I was in trouble. The sheriff called into the office on his walkie-talkie and told them to go get Joe. He then loaded the man into the back of his squad car and drove him on to Las Vegas so the authorities could book him for assault. I sure was lucky that Sheriff Tomes came along Route 25.

Joe fixed the flat, drove me home, and when we got out to go into the apartment, I fell flat on my face. There wasn't a warning. I just crumpled to the ground. So I spent last night in the hospital after the doctor ran tests to find out what was wrong with me. Other than being anemic, he said the tests looked fine. He prescribed an iron supplement and suggested lots of bed rest for the week.

"Wait a minute. What's with the man in the red sports car? Who does he think is, treating our mama like that?" I exclaimed.

"I know. Mom was lucky that the sheriff came along to save her. I loved that she was singing *Danny Boy*. That's one of my favorites too. Aunt Thelma used to sing it to me when I was little. She said she used to sing it to Mom. Do you know the song?" Cara asked.

"No, I can't say that I do, but I would like to have you sing it to me right now. I'm getting tired and would love to hear you sing me a song before I go to sleep. Tomorrow, I want to go run around the campus. I love to run, and Mom seemed to love to run before she got sick." I replied.

I went to sleep with a smile on my face as Cara sang "Danny Boy!"

December 25, 1955

Joe and I decided to get married exactly one year ago today. Even though our life has been a little rough financially, we are happy.

Mr. Ortiz is back in town full time, so Joe wants to go back to school with me next semester. We will have to sit down after the new year and see if we will have enough money for the tuition. We will pray that it all works out.

January 5, 1956

Our plans aren't going to work out after all. The new cafe manager in La Mesa is not working out, so Mr. Ortiz gave Joe a choice. He could either stay in Whistle Stop and run the cafe, or we would have to move to La Mesa and manage the new one. We opted to stay put so that we wouldn't have to move, and I wouldn't have to drive farther than I was already driving to school.

Joe is so good-natured. He wants me to read my required class assignments out loud to him so that he can learn along with me. What a man!

March 3, 1956

Life, precious life! Oh, how I wish that the love of my life were still here beside me! My Joe is gone. He was tragically taken away from me exactly a month ago today when he was on his way to the cafe after picking up a few supplies from the general store in town. Mr. Thompson opened the story early for Joe so the Men's League could have their weekly breakfast. One of the refrigerators quit working over the weekend, and Joe wasn't sure what was still edible, so he trekked down to the store to get just what he needed for the morning event.

Apparently, he decided to take a shortcut and walk along the train tracks on his way back. The early morning train that usually only goes from Albuquerque to Santa Fe on weekdays continued on to Las Vegas so that some artifacts could be sent on by truck to a festival outside of Cleveland. As Joe was stepping over one of the rails, his left foot got trapped in the railing. The sun had not come up yet, so the engineer didn't see him on the tracks.

I heard the train whistle as it came through Whistle Stop and wondered why there was a train that early on a weekday. Little did I know that Joe was on the track at the time the train whistle blew.

We had a closed casket funeral for Joe three days later. I didn't know much about his family, so we had a small memorial service at the cemetery with several folks from town. Aunt Thelma and Juan had to practically carry me to and from the car. I could not believe I was having to say good-bye to my husband. We had not been married a year. Life is not good right now.

I stopped going to school and haven't had the desire to return. It is difficult for me to function in daily life. Just getting out of bed and dressed for the day is monumental to me. Everywhere I go, everything I see reminds me of my sweet Joe.

Aunt Thelma has talked me into going on a trip back to Truway to see my Aunt Lottie. Aunt Lottie supposedly needs someone to help her schedule hair appointments at the Big Southern Hair Beauty Salon. Business has really picked up, and she says she really needs me to organize her schedule. I am going to go. For how long, I don't know. My energy level is lower than it ever has been. Another doctor's appointment is a must, but I will wait until I get to Texas to find out what's going on with me.

I stopped reading and stared at Cara for several minutes. We didn't say anything. We just looked at each other, searching for the right words to describe how we felt. Within a few minutes, which seemed like eternity, we started crying. What a terrible way to lose a soul mate. Poor Mama. How could she even function after losing Daddy like that?

Cara reached up and wiped away my tears, and I did the same for her. We decided that we would stop reading for the day and go to the library to research the plant life around El Paso. Not that I cared one bit about the plant life around here but Cara did. Maybe she will run with me in the morning before we start reading the diary again.

Jean and Jas Luke

Your word is a lamp to guide my
feet and a light for my path.

—Psalm 119:105 (NIV)

March 17, 1956

I made it back to Truway. Today I started my new job as the receptionist for the Big Southern Hair Beauty Salon. My aunt Lottie welcomed me with a sign on the front window that read "The Big Southern Hair Salon Welcomes Home Jean Louise Smallwood!"

    Aunt Lottie has made a big deal about me being in Truway and working in the salon, but I really wish that I could have had some more time alone. I guess being busy is good medicine for a broken heart, and busy is exactly what it is in the salon. Gertrude Jones came in to get her weekly rinse. She has a kind spirit, but she also likes to gossip, so I am sure that even the people who do not frequent Big Southern Hair will hear about my arrival. I know she will definitely tell her daughter, Bernice, that I am back. Bernice and I didn't get along well in high school. She had a major crush on Jas Luke Chilacothe and tried like the dickens to break us up many times. She would spread rumors that she and Jas Luke were secretly dating each other. My friends would come to me and say, "Did you hear the news?" I almost believed the first rumor I heard, but after the first, I never fell for the stories again. She was desperate to end our relationship! She was unsuccessful, but his mom sure wasn't. Oh, well, that's all history.

March 18, 1956

I am really tired. Aunt Lottie has scheduled a doctor's visit for me next week to see if I need iron tablets again or something. It's probably the stress and the long travel time. Maybe tomorrow, I will have more energy and not be so melancholy.

March 20, 1956

Phew! The days at the salon go by so fast. I have been going to bed the last two nights without writing, but I had to write tonight!

I was talking on the phone while trying to reschedule a weekly customer when the bell above the front door rang. I was engrossed in my duties as a receptionist, so I did not see who walked in, but when I heard, "Hello, Jean," my heart stopped beating for a second, and I froze. Within a few seconds, I confirmed the appointment and hung up, only to raise my head and stare into the eyes of Jas Luke Chilacothe. Oh my, he was even better looking than the last time I saw him on graduation night two years ago.

I said hello to him and asked why he wasn't in Boston going to school, and he said that his grandfather passed away last week. He came home for the funeral and to help his dad with the farm responsibilities for a couple of weeks. His grandfather had been his dad's partner and very active right up until the end.

It was so good to see Jas Luke. He asked if I would have lunch with him just to catch up. I hesitated at first because I didn't think it would be appropriate for a married woman to have lunch with an old boyfriend, but then I remembered that I wasn't married anymore. My Joe was gone. I thought it might be a good idea to have lunch with an old friend, so lunch it is at Della's Diner.

March 21, 1956

My lunch with Jas Luke was amazing. Not only did he listen intently when I told him about my adventures in Whistle Stop, going to school, meeting Joe and eventually marrying him, his eyes welled up with tears when I told him about Joe's death.

He shared his college stories with me, and we both laughed when he told about his fraternity initiation his first semester. It was a good, deep belly laugh. I don't think I have even smiled in the last two months.

Jas Luke walked me back to the salon and even scheduled a haircut for the next day with Aunt Lottie. We don't get too many men in for haircuts, so it is always a big event, especially when it's one of the handsome ones.

March 22, 1956

Jas Luke came into the salon, and my heart skipped a beat. He smiled at me, told me it was good to see me again. I reminded him that he just saw me yesterday. He said, "Jean, I could see you every day and still not see you enough."

I was relishing in his comment when Bernice Jones, Gertrude Jones's daughter, walked in and shrilled, "Jas Luke, what are you doing in the Big

Southern Hair Beauty Salon? You said that you were going to call me as soon as your grandfather's funeral was over, but I never heard from you. Not that I spend my time waiting by the phone for anyone to call me. My calendar is extremely busy every day, but I did think you were going to call since you told me you were going to call, and you didn't. I never thought I would see you in here! Why are you here?"

Before Jas Luke could answer, I said, "Hello, Bernice. Do you have an appointment? I don't seem to have you listed today."

"No, Jean, I'm not here for an appointment. I was on my way to Della's Diner and saw Jas Luke come in here, so I had to find out why he would be here of all places. Men don't come into the Big Southern Hair Beauty Salon!"

Jas Luke replied, "I'm a man, and I'm here to get my hair cut."

Bernice blushed three shades of red and apologized. Jas Luke told her that he needed to keep his appointment and excused himself. With Jas Luke gone, Bernice turned and walked out the door.

When he finished with his haircut, he walked to the front door, paused, looked back, and said, "Until we meet again."

Tomorrow, I will go to the doctor to see what is going on with me. I hope getting some iron tablets will do the trick.

"You know, Cara, Austin's mom is called Bernice. I wonder if this is the same person. Truway is so small, it's got to be the same one," CJ remarked as she paused before reading again.

March 23, 1956

I am in shock! When Dr. Thompson told me why I was feeling so tired, I couldn't speak. I am pregnant! Dr. Thompson prescribed vitamins for me to take and asked me to return in two weeks to see how I am doing.

Walking back to the salon, I passed by the Truway General Store and noticed a doll dressed up in the prettiest floral outfit with a matching hat for Easter. I had to stop and gaze at that doll in her beautiful clothes. I will be dressing up my baby in less than nine months. Dr. Thompson thinks the baby will be born in mid to late October.

If only Joe were still alive to share this magical time with me. I hope that our baby will look just like him. I waited until we were closing up the salon to tell Aunt Lottie the news. She grabbed me and hugged me and started crying. Of course, I began to cry too, but this time, they were tears of joy. There would be a new life in our family soon. I am going to write Aunt Thelma and let her know the news tomorrow. What a glorious day!

April 1, 1956

Believe it or not, I haven't given Jas Luke a thought in the last week, but not only did he walk into the salon today and ask me to go to lunch with him again, he told me he had something to tell me. I was curious, so I said I could get away today for a quick lunch with him.

We went to Della's Diner and sat in our old favorite booth in the back. He told me that he wasn't going back to Boston, and it was not an April's Fool joke. He was going to take the spring and summer off to help his dad and then return next fall. I was impressed with his obligation to his family. It could not be easy to give up a whole semester of work. He wanted to know if I would eat lunch with him every Friday until he left town. I sighed and almost told him about my baby-to-be, but instead, I found myself saying, "I will be glad to eat with you every Friday." Jas Luke gave me one of his biggest smiles as he turned and walked away.

I don't know why I didn't tell Jas Luke about the baby. I will but not today, maybe next Friday.

May 1, 1956

Not only am I having one baby—I am having two! Twins. I cannot believe it. It is definitely time to tell Jas Luke about my pregnancy. I am sure he will wonder why I kept it a secret for so long. My weekly lunch date with him is something I look forward to, and I guess I kept my predicament a secret because I am afraid he won't have lunch with me anymore.

I can tell that he is smitten with me again after all this time, and I have to admit, I feel the same way about him, but it's not fair to lead him on. He deserves a woman whom he can love, marry, and have children with. He surely will not want to take on a wife and some other man's children. It's just not fair to him. So I plan to tell him about the twins. He will be back at school when they are born, and I can send him a birth announcement.

"Whoa, CJ, can you believe everything we just read?" I jumped up and asked.

CJ had turned the reading over to me. CJ replied, "I know. I can hardly wait to see how she tells Jas Luke about us! I wonder if he will continue to see Mama once she tells him."

"I believe he loves Mom and will always love her whether she is having babies or not. He seems to be a gallant man. Let's keep reading and find out," I told her.

May 2, 1956

Well, knock me over with a feather! Not only did Jas Luke get wide-eyed about my news, he walked over and sat beside me in the booth and said, "Jean, I was waiting to find the right time to ask you this, but given your news, the time is now. Will you marry me?"

I didn't know what to say. Everything was happening so fast. Joe has only been gone for three months. I just found out about having twins, and now Jas Luke wants to marry me. It is too soon to marry someone else, but my feelings for Jas Luke never completely went away. and I have two babies to consider. so I found myself saying, "Of course I will."

We decided that we needed to get married right away, but when we went to tell our folks, his mother had other ideas. She said that everyone in their family had to have a farm wedding with all the trimmings, and it would take time to plan for such an event.

Jas Luke and I set up a time to tell his mother and father about his soon to be ready-made family. I only hope his mother doesn't try to stop the wedding from happening.

May 10, 1956

What a Mother's Day it has been. Jas Luke picked me up and took me on a picnic. He brought everything— food, grape juice to toast our upcoming marriage, and a book about the love of mothers.

We were so happy and decided it was time to break the news to his mother and father. Not a good idea. Jas Luke's mother wailed when he told her about the babies. She said she couldn't believe that we ruined her Mother's Day with such tragic news.

We wanted to get married on July 4, but his mother said that not only was that not enough time to prepare everything for the wedding, she thought it only best that we wait until after the babies were born. Most mothers would want a son to marry a woman *before* the babies arrived, but since they weren't Jas Luke's babies, Mrs. Chilacothe decided that it was only proper to wait so that I would not be pregnant in any of the wedding pictures.

Since she wasn't throwing a fit, we set the wedding date for November 1, 1956. Maybe Jas Luke's mother will soften once she sees the twins.

June 5, 1956

Today is my birthday, and do you know who else has a birthday today? Mrs. Chilacothe. Jas Luke has invited me to dinner at their house to celebrate our birthdays. Here's hoping that she will be glad to see me and embrace our birthday connection.

June 19, 1956

The workers on the farm had a presummer festival today. It was so much fun to join their eating, dancing, and the celebration of the farm. By this time next year, we will be celebrating with our own family during their festival.

Time is extremely busy right now. I am starting to grow. Everyone in Truway now knows about the babies and my marriage plans for November.

I am still working in the salon, seeing Jas Luke almost every day, and going to the doctor to see how the twins are doing. Life is good again.

September 7, 1956

The summer flew by with so many things going on. We just had the annual Chilacothe Summer Festival for the fiftieth year. What a celebration!

Dr. Thompson said that my babies might come early since they are twins, so he said it was time to stop working and get more rest. He said I would have plenty to do once the babies arrive.

Aunt Lottie fixes me lunch every day. She is doing double duty until she finds someone to take my place as receptionist at the salon. I feel so blessed to have not one but two aunts who love me like they do! My life is so full of wonderful, caring people. My babies will be surrounded by their love.

October 9, 1956

Oh, glorious day! My babies were born at five this morning. Two beautiful baby girls are now a part of my life. I just knew they were girls. Ever since I saw the doll in the Truway General Store, I had a feeling that I'd have baby girls. I have decided to call the one born first, Cora, Cora Jean. The first time I saw her face, I knew she was the "core" of my existence. I decided to call her sister, Cara, Cara Louise. I named her Cara because it means she is the special one who came out next. Cora and Cara, I love you so very much.

If only your daddy had lived to see you.

"Oh, how I wish our daddy could have seen us, CJ," I said as I took a deep breath.

"He would have loved us as much as Mama. I would have loved to watch him make his food creations," CJ remarked.

"Well, we'll have a different man bringing us up now that Mom is marrying Jas Luke. I hope he will love us like a daddy would," I said.

October 11, 1956

I brought the girls home from the hospital today. Aunt Lottie closed the salon for the rest of the week so she can take care of me, Cora, and Cara personally.

Jas Luke's mother has surprised us all by announcing that she wants her house people to help take care of me and the girls. Once I get on my feet, she said that I can help her plan the family meals and be on site as the wedding gets closer. It's already less than a month away. I don't want to leave Aunt Lottie, but I would be leaving her soon anyway, so next week, I will be unofficially a part of the Chilacothe family.

I can hardly wait to write Aunt Thelma and let her know about the girls' new homecoming. Maybe Aunt Thelma will be able to come for the wedding and see the girls at the same time. It will be so wonderful to see Aunt Lottie and Aunt Thelma in the same state at the same time. They have both been the most instrumental people in my life, and it is only right that I share Cora and Cara with them.

October 22, 1956

The girls are doing so well. They smile every time they hear my voice. I get to spend the majority of my time with them but have started helping the cook with planning and cooking the family meals. Even Mrs. Chilacothe has taken an interest in helping prepare the meals on occasion. Just this morning, she made breakfast and brought it to my room on a tray. She smiled at me, and I tried to smile back, but I know the smile melted off my face because even though she was smiling, her eyes looked cold and sinister. I shivered but found my voice to thank her for the breakfast. She is trying.

Speaking of trying, surprisingly, Bernice Jones visited me yesterday and brought me a box of chocolates and said she was so happy for Jas Luke and me. She said she knew we had never been friends in the past, but she sure hoped that now that we would both be living in Truway, we could spend more time getting to know one another. I guess I misjudged her.

October 26, 1956

The wedding is exactly a week from today. I am so excited! However, for the past three days, I have felt really bad by the end of the day. I am nauseous, dizzy, and some of my hair is falling out. Could this be my hormones acting up after having the girls? I need to schedule a day to see Dr. Thompson.

October 31, 1956

It's Halloween, the day before my wedding. I feel like I have been tricked with the way I am feeling. It's definitely no treat. Dr. Thompson is coming to the house today because I am too weak to go to his office. We're supposed to have the rehearsal dinner tonight, but unless Dr. Thompson has a miracle drug, I just don't see that happening.

November 1, 1956

Today was supposed to be my wedding day, but we had to postpone it until I get to feeling better. Dr.

Thompson gave me some medicine that he hopes will make me stronger. He said I need to go to the hospital to run tests. As it is, I can't even get out of bed. It has taken me an hour just to write this much in my diary.

Jas Luke brought me my breakfast today and told me not to worry about the wedding. There would be another day for us to get married. He's been bringing most of my meals to me since I don't have the strength to go down to the dining room right now. I am worried that something serious is wrong with me. I don't feel like writing anymore.

Lou Ann Brown, my most trusted friend among those working for the Chilacothes, is on her way up to help me bathe and change my clothes. I think I will ask her to hold onto my diary until I get to feeling better.

Please, God, if something happens to me, empower Aunt Lottie and Aunt Thelma to make the right decisions for my Cora and Cara. Hopefully, I will feel better in the morning and realize this has just been a frightening nightmare.

"CJ, there are no more entries. What does that mean? Did she die the next morning?" I asked.

"Aunt Lottie said she died on November 2, so yes, it was the next morning after her last entry."

CJ said with a sigh. "I can't believe we found our mom, just to lose her again so soon!" I cried.

Letter from Aunt Thelma found at the back of Mama's diary:

October 15, 1956

My Dear Sweet Jean Louise,

It was so wonderful to get your announcement about the birth of Cora Jean and Cara Louise! I cannot wait to see their adorable little faces in person. Seeing them and being there in person for your wedding are the two most important events coming up in my life, so count me in to be the lady with the biggest smile on the bride's side at the wedding while holding one, if not both of her baby girls.

My hope is that when your life gets back to normal (whatever normal is), you will plan a visit to the ranch. Of course, you have more pressing matters on your plate right now, but the invitation to come to Las Bonitas is always open to you and your family. Maybe you can even drag along that sister of mine when you come.

You asked me if I think you are being disloyal to Joe's memory by marrying Jas Luke so soon. Jean, I say you have to do what's right for you and your baby girls, and if that means marrying a man who obviously never quit loving you, then more power to you. Joe would want those babies to have a father, and I am sure Jas Luke Chilacothe will make a good husband

and a terrific father. I trust your instincts and always have. You have me in your corner, but you know that!

I want to write more, but our Samantha is about to go into labor. Can you believe our precious Samantha is going to be a mama burro? I'm thinking about calling the baby Sam, whether it's a boy or a girl. What do you think? Anyway, I want to be in the barn to encourage Samantha during this time in her life, so I will close for now.

I will see you in less than two weeks. By then, you and Samantha will both be new moms!

Love from the ranch,
Aunt Thelma

Sally Jane Nelson and a Dress from Paris

Because judgment without mercy will be
shown to anyone who has not been merciful.
Mercy triumphs over judgment.

—James 2:13 (NIV)

Cara and I couldn't talk to one another after finishing our mama's diary entries. We were both overwhelmed by all we learned. To top it off, we found the letter Aunt Thelma wrote to Mama after we were born. Mama didn't mention Aunt Thelma's arrival in her diary, so I guess she died soon after her last entry.

We told each other yesterday that reading her words made us feel like we lost both of our parents at the same time. How many children lose both parents to tragic deaths before they even get a chance to meet them? The hurt in *our* hearts has to be the worst ever and will never go away. I can't even imagine the pain that Aunt Lottie and Aunt Thelma must have gone through.

In some ways, I think I understand a little more about why they both believed they needed something that belonged to Mama, and that's why they decided to split us up. I've tried to get Cara to tell me how she is feeling, but she keeps going off by herself to read or research things in the library. I need for her to talk to me. Bearing this heartbreak alone is just too much.

Maybe she will talk to me about what could have happened to Mama when she comes back to the room tonight. Tomorrow, we have to go through a new student orientation class led by Dean Wittingham and some of the students who have been at Greenway for a long time. We are supposed to get mentors—that is, older students who will help us with our transition from public schools to the more prestigious Greenway School for girls. We also found out that since we were given a special scholarship to Greenway, we will need to work two hours a day in the school cafeteria. We meet with our supervisor tomorrow morning at six before our orientation to find out what our work time and responsibilities will be.

I am not looking forward to tomorrow. Cara and I need more time together, just the two of us before we meet other people. Cara didn't get back to the room until almost nine o'clock.

"Cara, where have you been?"

"I am sorry to be out so long, CJ! I have been in the library since early this morning and lost track of time."

"What could you possibly be researching that took you all day?"

"Well, I'll tell you. I have been looking up lots of things— food poisoning, anemia, heart defects, and more about Marfan syndrome. I need answers to why our mom died. We were told that the doctor thought mom had an enlarged heart, and that caused her to get sick, but she was too young to die, even with an enlarged heart. Supposedly, I didn't inherit Marfan syndrome from Mom or Dad, but now I'm not so sure about that. I wish I could talk to Glen about Mom and my diagnosis. He knows a lot more than me about Marfan syndrome and its symptoms. I did tell you about Glen, right? Aren't you the least bit curious about what killed her?"

"Wait a minute, one question at a time. No, you did not tell me about Glen. Who is Glen? Yes, I am curious about what killed our mother, but until we have time to talk to the people who knew Mama the best, we will have to go on with our lives here at school. Our aunts want us here to get a good education so that we will amount to something. We'll have to put our Sherlock-and-Watson days on hold for now. Who is Glen?"

"Glen is a boy I met at the hospital when I had my eye surgery. He also has Marfan syndrome, and before you ask, no, he is not my boyfriend. He's just someone I met who has something in common with me, and I like to correspond with him on occasion. The confidence he has in himself has rubbed off on me. I am now able to embrace Marfan syndrome and see it as a blessing rather than a curse. If I didn't have Marfan, I wouldn't have met Glen," Cara responded.

"Wow, it is so cool that you write letters to a boy. I can't wait to hear more about this mysterious Glen. However, I want you to think about something, Cara. Aunt Lottie and Aunt Thelma said that Mama seemed to get tired easily, especially after she left Truway and went to live in New Mexico. Dr. Thompson offered to do an autopsy, but both of our aunts couldn't deal with that, so they took his word for it. The death certificate said she died from complications with her heart. She basically had a heart attack at the age of twenty-one."

Cara sighed. "I don't believe she just died with heart complications. I think something happened to cause her death, and as soon as this year's over, I plan to research more and investigate what happened to Mom. Why did she want Lou Ann Brown to keep her diary? Why not just put it by her bed until the next day? Did she suspect that someone she knew was trying to harm her? All the people in her life at the time seemed to love her, so could she have died from natural causes? There are too many unanswered questions that we need to find out about. This summer, I want to go to Truway and see where you found the diary. Maybe we will find another clue behind the brick in the cellar, maybe a note or something that was hidden with the diary. Let's just go to bed now. We can talk about all of this later."

And later never came. We called Aunt Lottie to tell her that everything was going okay at school, but that we wanted to come home during out next break to investigate what might have happened to Mama. Aunt Lottie said, "Please don't do this to yourself, CJ. Your mom died of natural causes. She would want you and Cara to focus on your education and spend as much time as possible with each other."

Maybe Aunt Lottie was right. Maybe we were making a mountain out of a molehill. Mama would want us to concentrate on school.

Our first official day was extremely busy. First, we had a meeting with our breakfast supervisor, Mrs. Oates. Cara and I would both be working the 6–8 a.m. shift behind the food line in the Eugene Nelson Cafeteria. She said that we would also have a chance to work with the food service team during special functions hosted by organizations at school.

Then we spent time in the Greenway orientation, which was not very helpful. The mentors weren't upper classmen. They were girls our own age who have been at Greenway since first grade and volunteered to be mentors to new students.

Their names are Freda Gates, Sheila Sue Marx, Bobbie Jo Turner, and Sally Jane Nelson. Bobbie Jo Turner will be mine and Cara's mentor for the semester. She seems nice, but she sure does rely on Sally Jane Nelson to tell her what to do. Freda and Sheila relied on Sally Jane's cues too. They all have two girls to mentor so that makes eight new girls at Greenway. Hopefully, we will have time between our work schedule and our classes to bond with our new classmates. Something tells me that we don't measure up to the longtime residents' standards, but who cares. I am sure they are way too busy to worry about us interfering with any of their plans anyhow.

All the mentors belong to a sorority called Alpha Tau Zeta, and that's what they talked about the most. They invited us to their ice cream social, a get-to-know-you time in the Alpha Tau Zeta drawing room tonight right after dinner. Of course, that is one of the special organization functions that Cara and I have to work at, so I guess we won't be attending as guests. Being a member of a sorority is not on my list of priorities because I really don't know what's so great about being a member of a sorority in the first place. Time will tell.

We were escorted to dinner by Bobbie Jo. She was pleasant enough, but even though she was talking to us, her eyes were watching everything Sally Jane was doing at the next table. When dinner was over, everyone got up to go change for the ice cream social. We still wore our dress slacks and the Greenway School for girls' polo shirts on that we received in our registration packet because we knew we would have to wear white linen aprons over our clothes when serving others.

Mrs. Oates ushered us into the kitchen beside the drawing room and told us to scoop vanilla ice cream into crystal parfait glasses. We spooned chocolate sauce over the ice cream and added a cherry to the top of more than fifty ice cream sundaes. Next, we put parfaits on trays and carried them out to the drawing room to serve to the girls after the welcome given by none other than Sally Jane Nelson.

I decided to load up my tray and serve as many people as possible, as quickly as possible so I could go back out and meet some new people. So I kept adding sundaes to my tray until there wasn't room for any more. Of course, Cara only put a few on her tray. I would have my parfaits served and ready to come back to fix my own sundae before Cara got through serving hers. I guess I would be a nice sister and fix her ice cream sundae for her while I waited for her to finish serving.

The tray seemed heavy when I picked it up, but I took a big breath, made sure I had the tray balanced, and took off to go through the swinging door to the drawing room. I was thinking about how wonderful my ice cream sundae was going to taste once I served everyone. Just as I was through the swinging door, one of the new girls came barreling toward me to get her parfait glass off my tray. Before I could tell her to hold on, she was grabbing not one, but two sundaes off the tray.

My tray started leaning, and gravity just took over. The tray took on a personality of its own. Instead of falling to the floor with me, it flipped up in the air slinging ice cream with chocolate sauce and cherries everywhere. There were girls screaming, some were laughing, others were crying, but one in particular, Sally Jane Nelson, was screeching at the top of her lungs. "YOU HAVE RUNIED MY PARIS DRESS!"

Instead of apologizing like I should have, I asked the dumbest question. "Is your dress from Paris, France, or Paris, Texas?"

I didn't get to eat my ice cream sundae and neither did Cara. School started and our semester was over before we knew it.

We don't get to serve at the next function, the end-of-year dance. We have to wash dishes in the kitchen and clean up the drawing room after the dance is over. Poor Cara. She didn't even do anything wrong, but because she is related to me, she is being punished. She told me that she would rather be working with me in the kitchen than being out where the girls would be flirting with boys from Montgomery Bell School from across town.

We are not supposed to set foot in the drawing room. Alpha Tau Zeta transformed it into a party room with shimmery streamers hanging from the ceiling and a mirrored

126

spinning ball in the middle of the room. I heard some of the girls talking about how the ball will shed light across the room as it turns, and all the other lights will be off.

I am standing at the kitchen window, watching as the sorority girls try to keep their balance in their high-heeled shoes as they walk up the steps of the Alpha Tau Zeta building. Their dresses are amazing.

I was wondering how many of their ball gowns came from Paris when I noticed a bus in front of the building. The bus doors opened, and out came boys of all shapes and sizes dressed in their Sunday best. Some of them even had on different colored tuxedos. My mouth flew open, and I craned my neck to get a better look at one of the boys getting off the bus.

It was Austin, Austin Chilacothe! He was right here in El Paso going to an all boys' school just as Cara and I are going to an all girls' school. Imagine that.

"Cara, you are not going to believe *who* I just saw!"

"I can't guess who it might be, CJ, so you will just have to tell me," Cara said.

"It's Austin Chilacothe from Truway. He's been one grade below me since I was in first grade, and he's here going to school. He got off that bus parked in front of the building, so he must go to Montgomery Bell School. I need to at least say hello since we have known each other for so long."

"CJ, you can't go say hi to Austin. We are not allowed in the drawing room tonight. We have to stay in the kitchen and prepare all the food and drinks," Cara exclaimed.

"Oh, baloney sandwiches, I have to say hello. What if I wait to see where he goes when he's inside, and when he's standing alone, I can carry a tray out like I know what I'm doing.

"That plan makes me nervous, CJ. If someone sees you out of the kitchen, it could mean the end of our jobs and maybe even the end of our days at Greenway. It would hurt Aunt Lottie and Aunt Thelma so much if we get kicked out of school before our classes even get started."

"I will be discreet, Cara. I will wait until the evening is almost over," I told her.

That ridiculous dance went on for two more hours before I heard silence in the drawing room. I boldly took one of the trays without anything on it and pushed through the swinging door.

If I hadn't stopped to make sure I wasn't running into anyone, I would have run smack into Austin. He was standing outside the swinging door just as I was coming out. He had a shocked look on his face, just like someone had thrown him a surprise birthday party, but he slowly gave me his Austin grin. "CJ, what are doing here?" Austin asked.

"I'm going to school here."

"Well, if you're going to school here, why are you carrying a tray and wearing an apron?"

"Cara and I work here to help pay our tuition, and we were assigned to helping with the dance tonight."

"Who's Cara?" he continued with his line of questions.

"Cara is my twin sister. I thought you knew that I had a sister. Aunt Lottie sent me here to go to school with Cara who's been growing up in New Mexico on a ranch."

"That's groovy, CJ! Does she look like you?" Austin asked his fourth question of the evening.

"No, we are not identical. Would you like to meet her? She's in the kitchen."

"Sure," he replied, finally no more questions.

We went into the kitchen together, and I introduced him to Cara. She blushed when he said hello to her. She is a little shy with most folks, but I guess a good-looking boy would make anyone blush. Austin is the best-looking boy I have ever seen, and I looked at all the boys who got off the Montgomery Bell bus.

Cara told Austin about how we got to see each other after all of these years, and she told him how much she loves spending time with me. She told him all about the Las Bonitas Ranch, Aunt Thelma, and Sam, the white burro. She even told him about Marfan syndrome, only because Austin remarked about her long fingers. I love Cara's response to Austin. "The better to type research papers with, my dear." She laughed.

I got so caught up in listening to everything she was telling Austin that I didn't hear anyone else coming into the kitchen until I heard Sally Jane screech. "Austin Chilacothe, why are you in the kitchen with the help?" Sally Jane began her own line of questioning.

"I didn't realize you were looking for me, Sally Jane. How did you know I was here?" Austin asked her.

"Freda said she was watching you and saw you talking to CJ, and then she saw you go into the kitchen with her. Why would you want to see a kitchen?" Sally Jane kept it up.

"CJ and I are both from Truway. We have been in school together since we were very small, so we were just saying hello to each other. This is CJ's twin sister, Cara. She's the reason I came into the kitchen."

"I know CJ and Cara, Austin. After all, we are in the same school." Sally Jane retorted.

"Well, seeing as how you weren't acknowledging either one of them, I thought you might need to be properly introduced or something," Austin added.

I must have been smiling at Austin's comment because Sally Jane snorted. "I don't need you to introduce me to anyone at my own school, Austin. I think your bus is about to leave. I asked you to dance with Freda before you left, but now the band has stopped playing, and you won't get that chance."

"Oh, darn." Austin had that sheepish grin on his face.

"Austin Chilacothe, if you weren't my cousin, I would never speak to you again." And with that, Sally Jane turned and headed toward the door. When she was about to push through the door, Freda and the rest of the Sally Jane Fan Club fell into the kitchen. They must have been eavesdropping on our conversation and tried to move out of the way when they heard Sally Jane's comment so close to the door. In all the commotion, the door smacked Sally Jane in the head.

"Freda, what is the matter with all of you? I told you I would come in here to get Austin. I didn't need you and the other girls to come looking for me. Now look what you've done? I can't face Benjamin Bookman with this huge bump on my head. CJ, get an ice bag out of the refrigerator for me."

Austin grabbed my arm as I turned to go to the refrigerator and said, "No, CJ, I will get my cousin some ice for her head. It's not your responsibility to wait on her."

Austin got the ice, Sally Jane put it on her head, and the whole entourage walked out of the kitchen with Sally Jane leading the pack. Austin was the caboose, and as he was nearing the door, he turned and smiled at me and said, "CJ, it sure was a pleasure seeing you tonight. It was the highlight of the whole evening. Cara, I want the opportunity to hear more about you, Sam, and the Las Bonitas Ranch. Maybe both of you could come to my birthday party in Truway this summer. I'll send you an invitation."

I smiled at him and continued to smile the entire time we spent cleaning up the Alpha Tau Zeta drawing room. Austin Chilacothe is Sally Jane's cousin? How about that? We certainly live in a small world. What an exciting night this has been even though I didn't get to do any dancing in a Paris dress.

New Mexico Bound

Look straight ahead, and fix your
eyes on what lies before you.

—Proverbs 4:25 (NIV)

Summer is here, and we planned to go to Truway to visit Aunt Lottie and attend Austin's birthday. We also hoped to investigate Mom's death; however, we had to change our plans because Aunt Thelma took a spill off her horse and broke her leg. She sent Juan to pick us up on the last day of school. CJ and I are more than happy to help Aunt Thelma with the ranch for awhile. Maybe before the summer is over, we can talk her into going to Truway with us.

The ride to the Las Bonitas Ranch was long and dusty, but we finally made it just as the sun was setting over the mountains. "I thought we had beautiful sunsets in Texas, but this sunset in the New Mexico desert is spectacular!" CJ marveled.

As much as I wanted to get out of the car and see Sam, there was no way I was going to venture out in the dark tonight. Morning would be here before we knew it, and besides, Aunt Thelma would be waiting for us in the house.

I got to see Sam first thing the next morning. His love for me is touching. As soon as he heard my voice, he ran toward us and nudged my hand. When CJ said hello to him, he raised his head and nodded at her. "Imagine a burro who practically talks with his head! I feel like I have known you my whole life, Sam, the Snow-White Burro," CJ told him. She immediately knelt down beside him, hugged his neck, and started caressing his head, ears, and face.

As soon as the ranch chores were taken care of, CJ and I went for a horseback ride and saw most of the ranch. I had forgotten how beautiful the ranch was. It was great to be home.

After our horseback ride and a lunch of chicken tortilla soup, Aunt Thelma wanted us to see her artifact collection.

"Your mom loved my artifact collection! I truly believe that had she lived to be an old lady like me, she would have organized the pieces so that she could start a museum on the ranch. As soon as you get settled, I would like for Juan to drive us to the Whistle Stop Cafe for breakfast and then drive us into Las Vegas to eat lunch at another famous restaurant in Northeast New Mexico—Charlie's Spic & Span—which features handmade burritos. I know what Cara's favorite food is, but what is your favorite food, CJ?"

"Mine would be French fries, but burritos would be a close second," I told her.

"Well, Charlie's burritos are world famous, so you're in luck. After we eat lunch, we'll go visit many of the historical sites around Las Vegas. One of which is the Santa Fe Trail Interpretive Art Center. The Las Vegas history is very interesting. This area was once a place where twenty-one Rough Riders, led by Theodore Roosevelt, charged up San Juan Hill. But as tough a town as it was, Las Vegas also became a town of sophistication. Like a cross between Tucson and New York, Las Vegas had gunslingers, like Jesse James and Doc Holliday's Saloon and the upper crust of society in the opera houses. Las Vegas was like an oasis in the desert; it drew people with money and influence."

"A combination of things ended Las Vegas's stint in the spotlight. Agriculture took a big hit during the Dust Bowl years. The Depression also contributed to its decline. But its biggest downfall was the same thing that had originally built it—the lack of people riding the railroad." Aunt Thelma's passion for Las Vegas was evident as she described its story.

The next morning came very early since we stayed up late to talk about school, the ranch, and our parents. Aunt Thelma told us about our dad's cooking talents, so I was more than excited to find out about the Mexican cuisine dishes he was famous for at the Whistle Stop Cafe. We planned to eat breakfast there and then drive to Las Vegas. I could tell that I would have to run a few miles each morning to burn the calories from the food I was going to be eating. It amazed me how Cara could eat as much as she does without exercising but still seemed to maintain her weight.

Mr. Ortiz greeted us as soon as we entered the cafe. "Hello, Thelma! Who are these beautiful young women with you?"

"You know Cara, Roberto. The girl beside her is her sister, Cora Jean, whom we lovingly call CJ. They're here for the summer to help me out at the ranch. They're interested in hearing about Joe's specialty dishes that you still have on the menu."

"Jean's delight is probably the most requested. It is a mixture of eggs, cream cheese, green chilies, potatoes, tomatoes, and onions wrapped in one of our homemade flour tortillas," Mr. Ortiz described.

"Is Jean's delight named after our mom?" CJ asked.

"It sure is!" he exclaimed.

"Then I definitely want to order Jean's delight. Thank you very much!" CJ added.

"Cara, do you want your usual, Joes breakfast taco?"

"Yes, please," I responded.

Aunt Thelma told Mr. Ortiz she also wanted Joe's breakfast Taco.

Knowing that two of the breakfast entrees at the Whistle Stop Cafe were named after our parents is so meaningful. Sharing a time to eat them with CJ and Aunt Thelma is unforgettable.

Before we left, Mr. Ortiz told us the history of the Whistle Stop Cafe and gave a special personal invitation to take part in the fiftieth anniversary celebration, which will be held the summer of 1978. We will have to make sure that we are around to be in Whistle Stop for this memorable occasion.

Our day did not end until ten o'clock at night. CJ and I ate at Charlie's Spic & Span and toured Las Vegas. Aunt Thelma had Juan drive us to the Heritage Days fairgrounds before leaving.

"Girls, I need a big favor from both of you. I usually lead the Heritage Days grand entry parade from the fairgrounds, but with this broken leg, I just don't think I will be able to get my riding in and be ready to lead the other riders for the parade. Do you think you could take my place this year since you'll be here for Heritage Days?" Aunt Thelma asked.

"We would love to take your place, right, Cara? But what is Heritage Days all about?" CJ inquired.

"The Heritage Days Festival features *Places with a Past*," I told CJ.

"In addition to the parade, there are tours of the historic places in town, and the festival features hundreds of booths set up by vendors from all over New Mexico and Arizona. Booths showcasing some of the most talented Hispanic and Native American artists who have dedicated their lives to making award winning jewelry, paintings, and pottery," Aunt Thelma continued.

"We should also set up a booth and display some of the artifacts you have, Aunt Thelma." CJ recommended.

"Actually, I have always wanted to make my own pottery. Remember when we said that someday we would make our own pottery, Cara? I think it's time," Aunt Thelma said.

"I do. Do you think we have enough time to make one or two between now and the first weekend in August?" I asked.

"We could give it a try. Let's go buy a potter's wheel, some clay, and paint before going back to the ranch," Aunt Thelma commented.

The next morning, CJ walked toward me as I was pouring a glass of orange juice in the kitchen. "Cara, look what I found in Mama's keepsake box. I discovered a hidden drawer at the bottom of the box. I pushed up on the side and discovered this drawer. When I opened it, I found this," CJ gushed.

CJ opened her hand, and sitting in her palm was the most exquisite turquoise and coral ring. "This had to be Mom's wedding ring that Dad gave her. It once belonged to Dad's family, so there is no telling how old it is. I wonder who made it." I commented.

"Do you think Aunt Thelma would know?" CJ asked.

"Let's ask her," I replied. We went in search of our aunt and her knowledge about the ring.

Aunt Thelma knew a little about the history of the ring, but she thought it would be worth our while to visit with Mr. Ortiz to find out more about the ring and our dad's family.

He told us our great grandfather made the ring and gave it to his wife. The ring continued to be passed on to the next generation's oldest son to give to his betrothed. He told us that he didn't think anyone in our dad's family was still around, but he thought we might find out more by showing the ring to some of the vendors who would be taking part in the Las Vegas Heritage Week.

This summer has already started to be such a rewarding experience for both of us. We can't wait to see what else we find out about the ring.

"Cara, you definitely have a knack for making vases. You inherited the artistic blood from our dad's family. The wedding vase is absolutely amazing!"

"Thanks, CJ. I am rather fond of this vase too. I don't know if I want to sell it or not, but I made it for Heritage Days, so I need to follow through with the plan. Making a few extra dollars is going to be helpful for Aunt Thelma," Cara replied.

"Do you still want to take Sam with us so that people will see Dad's beautiful Indian blanket?" CJ asked.

"Of course. Sam loves to people watch, and his presence is an excellent way for us to advertise our wares," Cara explained.

August 1 came quicker than we expected. It was the day before Heritage Days, and we had to go into Las Vegas to set up our booth. Juan drove the trailer with Sam and the horses behind Aunt Thelma's truck. The truck had a camper attached. CJ and I planned to spend the night so that we could set up our booth. Another ranch hand called Bud drove Juan's truck so that Juan and Aunt Thelma could go back home tonight. Juan would drive her back to the fairgrounds tomorrow before the start of the parade.

As we pulled into our designated spot to set up camp, we saw many other vendors who had already arrived and had the same idea to spend the night on the grounds. We parked and got Sam out to take a stroll through the festival booths. We saw many Native Americans and others setting up their tables. The Navajo weavers were putting up their signs, and the Pueblo pottery makers were setting out some of their vases. There was one booth that had a sign which read "Jewelry by Joe."

"Hello there. Are you Joe by chance?" I asked.

"Yes, I am Joe, and my grandfather is also Joe. I even had an uncle named Joe, but he was killed in a tragic accident many years ago a few miles from here. Of course, I never got to meet him in person. My dad just told me he named me after my grandfather and his brother Joe," he replied.

"Really? My dad's name was Joe, and he too was killed in a train accident on the tracks behind the Whistle Stop Cafe in 1956."

"No way. That's how my uncle died. Could it be that we are talking about that same man?"

CJ and I turned and looked at each other. Could this guy be our cousin? Where have these relatives been all these years?

It was like Joe knew what I was thinking because he said, "My grandfather, my father, and I have been living in Santa Fe ever since I was born, but we decided to come out to the Heritage Days last year and find out more about my uncle's past. We spent time talking with the owner of Charlie Rose's Mexican restaurant, and he told us about Joe's move to Whistle Stop.

"We drove into the town and ate at the Whistle Stop Cafe before heading back to Santa Fe after the festival was over, but the owner was out of town, and the new manager did not know whether Joe had family in the area or not. He knew about Joe because we all ate Joe's breakfast taco. We thought it was pretty cool to know it was named after Uncle Joe, but that's as close as we got to knowing anything about him. We came back this year and thought we'd try to find out more about him."

I pulled out our mom's wedding ring and held it up for Joe to see. "Have you seen any other rings made like this one?"

"Yes, I have. We make a similar design and replicate it as much as possible to put into the shops in Santa Fe. We've been able to sell them as fast as we can make them. Where did you get this unique one? Does it have a mark on the inside of the band?"

I handed the ring to him so that he could inspect it closer. "Ah, here it is. See this mark? This is a mark that only my great-grandfather would put on his original jewelry pieces. This ring is actually just like the one he gave my great-grandmother when he asked her to marry him. Unfortunately, we don't know what happened to the ring. My dad said that Grandfather gave the ring to Uncle Joe, and he must have sold it when he was trying to make ends meet before landing the job as a chef in the cafe."

"No, he didn't sell it! This is the same ring!" I burst out as I walked closer to him.

"He gave it to our mom when he asked her to marry him. She died right after we were born, but we found the ring in a secret drawer in her keepsake box. You have to be our cousin, Joe! Our names are Cara and CJ" I continued.

"Well, I can't believe it. Come over to the camper and meet my grandfather, and not just mine but yours too," Joe motioned.

"Grandfather, look at this ring these girls showed me. Their names are Cara and CJ."

Our grandfather looked at the ring, looked at us, and then looked at the ring again. "Where did you girls find this ring?" he asked.

"It belonged to our mother, Jean. Our dad was Joe, the same Joe who invented Joe's breakfast taco," I replied.

Grandfather Joe stared at me and then turned and looked at CJ. He teared up but at the same time smiled and said, "You are an answer to prayer, young ladies. I knew Joe had to have met someone he spent time with before he left this earth. Knowing that you exist is even better. Joe had two girls? Which one of you is older?"

"We are twins, even though we don't look alike. Dad never got to meet us. We were born after he died, and our mom died a short while after we were born. We were raised by two great aunts in two different places and only met each other six months ago," I told him.

We stayed and had supper with our grandfather and cousin. Wait until Aunt Thelma comes tomorrow. She is not going to believe we found our dad's relatives.

Aunt Thelma was indeed surprised. She said she would love to meet him after the parade. CJ and I were announced as the grand marshalls for the parade. We rode side by side. Sam walked behind us. He walked with a prance in his steps like he knew he was showing off Dad's blanket. Everyone was smiling as we rode by, but not as much as our grandfather when we rode by him and our newfound cousin.

We had a great time visiting with the people who frequented our booths. Instead of selling the wedding vase, CJ and I decided to give it to Grandfather. As tears began to run down his face, he thanked us in a whisper and said, "Cara and CJ, my long-lost granddaughters, may you forever prosper as you continue life's journey."

What an adventure it has been in New Mexico. Aunt Thelma said that she will be strong enough to drive us to Truway next week. She hasn't been there since the fall of Mom's death. I will finally get to visit Truway!

Jewelry
by
Joe

Tales and Trepidations
in Truway, Texas

> Be kind and compassionate to one another forgiving
> each other, just as in Christ, God forgave you.
>
> —Ephesians 4:32 (NIV)

"Cara, can you believe how fast the summer has gone?"
I asked.

"No, I can't, and I'm so glad we are almost in Truway." Cara
stated.

Driving through town at dusk on an August evening with
Aunt Thelma was very special. Not only did I already have
a lot of emotion about returning to Truway, but seeing the

lights in store windows and on lamp posts outside the church and community center made me smile.

"CJ, it's beautiful here! No wonder you loved living here. I can understand why Mom wanted to return to Truway too, whenever she lost Dad," Cara said.

I will always love Truway and really don't want to leave again, but we will have to return to school in a few weeks. Someday I will return and stay.

"Thelma, Cara, CJ, you're finally here. I've been watching for you to pull up in front of the salon for over an hour. Did you see my sign?" she asked.

We turned toward the salon and saw, "Welcome, Thelma, Cara, and CJ!" draped across the salon's picture window. Aunt Lottie made a sign for us just like she did Mama.

"Hi, Aunt Lottie. It's so great to see you!" I heard Cara say as she and Aunt Thelma hugged her neck.

"We're glad we're finally here," I chimed in as I reached out to embrace Aunt Lottie too.

"Lou Ann, do you remember CJ?" Aunt Lottie turned and addressed a woman sitting at the reception counter as we walked into the salon.

"Of course. Hi, CJ. It's nice to see you again. And you must be Cara," Lou Ann said.

"Hi, Mrs. Brown. Yes, this is my sister, Cara. How are Emma Lou and Bea?" I asked.

Lou Ann walked toward us as she said, "Both girls are growing like weeds. They will be so happy to see you." She hugged me and then embraced Cara.

"It's going to be great to see them and catch up on what's been going on," I told her.

Aunt Lottie smiled at us and said, "Lou Ann has been working for me now. Not only is she the receptionist at the front, she also takes care of my books for the salon. My old eyes aren't what they used to be, so I decided to ask for help, and I'm blessed to have Lou Ann here."

Lou Ann looked at Aunt Lottie with such devotion. It made me happy to know she had someone who had her best interest at heart. I turned and looked at Cara to see if she was taking in the moment, and I was surprised to see her looking at me in a curious way. She kept darting her eyes over to where Lou Ann was sitting.

I knew she was trying to tell me something, but it would have to wait. Obviously, she didn't want Lou Ann nor Aunt Lottie to know what she was thinking. It's funny how Cara and I have been able to almost read each other's minds ever since we met. I guess that's a twin thing. I marvel at her on a daily basis and thank God that we have each other in our lives.

"Aunt Lottie, is it okay with you if we walk over to the house? I'm anxious to show it to Cara," I asked.

"Sure, you must be exhausted from your long trip. Here's the key. Make yourselves comfortable. Thelma, will you stay with me and help close the salon. We'll all eat the taco salad I made and share stories around the table later."

We didn't even get all the way out the door before Cara started talking excitedly. "CJ, do you know who Lou Ann is?"

"Of course, I know who she is. I have known her family for years." Then I continued, "Wait a minute. I know why you are so animated. Now that she is working for Aunt Lottie, we have the chance to question her about Mama's diary."

"We've got to talk to her and ask her more about hiding the diary and why she hid it rather than giving it to Aunt Lottie," Cara said.

We continued to talk about how wonderful it was to have Lou Ann Brown in our lives just when we needed to solve the mystery about what happened to our mother.

Having Aunt Lottie and Aunt Thelma in the same house at the same time was extra special. The taco salad was scrumptious. Cara and I looked forward to tomorrow as we lulled ourselves to sleep by singing "Danny Boy."

The next morning, Cara and I asked Aunt Lottie if it would be okay with her if we invited Lou Ann to lunch so we could ask her questions about her friendship with Mom.

"Lou Ann will enjoy going to lunch with you two. She always loved your mom. They had sleepovers many nights when they were in high school. Lou Ann married Jo Bob Brown right after they graduated from school. He is now the proud owner of his own farm. John Mark Chilacothe gave him the land where his house sits, as well as ten acres to farm.

"As a result, Lou Ann can work for me rather than working fourteen-hour days on the Chilacothe farm. After all these years, John Mark made good on his promise to give the house and land to Jo Bob. I am truly proud of John Mark!" Aunt Lottie sighed. She seemed to stare off into space for a moment and forget she was talking to us.

"Oh my. Listen to me carrying on like I have all the time in the world to chat. I wish I could take off a few days and spend time with you, but the hair dryers are calling me." Aunt Lottie laughed and walked away.

"You know, Cara, I think John Mark Chilacothe was once smitten with Aunt Lottie. I heard more than one conversation under the hair dryers about a fellow and Aunt Lottie. It just dawned on me that the 'smitten fellow' is John Mark Chilacothe. Did you see the way she looked when she was talking about him?" I asked.

"How about that? The Chilacothes and the Trinitys seem to have long-term relationships with each other, huh?" Cara said.

We went to the salon early to find out what time Lou Ann wanted to go to lunch. She said an early lunch was really the best because they were expecting several people from the ladies' auxiliary club to come in together for their weekly hair appointments. She went on to tell us they were going to honor Brother Mike in a special ceremony this evening at church.

"Who's Brother Mike?" Cara asked.

"Cara, Brother Mike is the reason I wrote you the letter over six months ago before we met each other. He is our longtime interim pastor at the church and an inspiration to this entire community," I said proudly.

"Can we go to the ceremony?" Cara asked Lou Ann.

"Of course you can, Cara. Brother Mike will be happy to see you," Lou Ann replied.

We walked over to Della's Diner and sat at the back in a secluded booth so that it would be difficult for someone to eavesdrop on our conversation. Cara and I decided it would be best for me to start the conversation since I was the one who knew Lou Ann and also the one who found the diary in the storm cellar.

"Lou Ann, thanks for having lunch with us. Taking you to lunch is our way of thanking you for the friendship you had with our mama," I told her.

"I loved your mama like a sister. I mourned her loss for a long time after she died. She was way too young to die," Lou Ann said.

"Would you tell us about the days before Mama's death? What was happening to her? What did she say to you? I want you to know that I found her diary in the storm cellar right before I left to meet Cara and go to school in El Paso. Cara and I read the diary together. We have been waiting for the right opportunity to come to Truway and find out what happened to Mama," I said very quickly.

"I'll tell you that your mama was courageous right up until the end. She had me bring both of you to her room every day that she was bedridden. She would bottle-feed one of you, and I would feed the other, then at the next bottle-feeding time, we would switch. She was very weak, so I stayed with her as much as possible the last couple of days," she explained.

"Why did she ask you to hide her diary?" Cara asked.

"She started having paranoid thoughts about someone trying to poison her the day before she died. She was afraid to write about it in her diary, but she told me that she believed she was being poisoned, and that she wanted me to hide the diary because she didn't want it to fall into the wrong hands," Lou Ann whispered to us.

"Poisoned?" I gulped.

"Yes. She never trusted Mrs. Chilacothe nor Bernice Jones. Both of them acted like they wanted to help your mama, but she was suspicious of their actions. Mrs. Chilacothe brought her breakfast each morning after your mother moved into the big house. Bernice brought her candy as a token of her friendship. Soon after, your mama got sick and was bedridden. Dr. Thompson said that she had a weak heart, and that's why she died. No one argued with him about her dying at such an early age. He was a trusted physician.

"I was not convinced, but you have to understand something. My husband and I worked for the Chilacothes. I had no proof. There was no evidence that there was foul play, so after awhile, I bought into the notion that Jean did have a weak heart and died as a result."

"Do you think it is possible that someone was trying to harm Mom?" I asked.

After a long pause, Lou Ann began shaking her head up and down. We ate our lunch in silence after we prayed for God to lead us to the truth about Mom.

The ceremony for Brother Mike was special. Cara and I stayed until everyone left so she could meet him. "Cara, we finally get to meet one another. You've been in my prayers on many occasions. You too, CJ," Brother Mike said.

"Thank you, Brother Mike. I could feel your prayers. We have one we would like for you to pray with us now," I told him.

CJ explained to him what we found out from Lou Ann and how we suspected something was amiss when we read her diary. He listened intently as we told him probably more than he wanted to hear.

Finally, he said, "Girls, I'll be glad to pray with you and ask God to help you find out what might have happened to your mom. I'll also pray that he'll give you discernment so that all the pieces of the puzzle can come into place without making rash judgments."

We bowed our heads and listened as Brother Mike asked God to watch over us and give us wisdom as to how to proceed with our investigation.

Austin's birthday celebration is tonight. Aunt Lottie said she and Aunt Thelma would drive us over to the Chilacothe's, but they didn't want to stay for the festivities.

"I haven't been in the Chilacothe house since I was a teenager, and I don't relish returning at this stage in my life," Aunt Lottie said.

I wondered how many times she visited the Chilacothes in her younger years but decided not to ask.

As soon as we walked into the front door of the big white house, I watched Cara's reaction to the grandeur of the place. "CJ, this house is amazing!" Cara exclaimed.

"I know, isn't it? I've only been here once, and that was just passing through to Emma Lou's house a few years back. We could live here and not see each other for days," I responded.

"Maybe we could sneak away after we sing "Happy Birthday" to Austin and see if we can figure out which room Mom stayed in," Cara pondered.

"How would we know which one it was?" I asked.

Just as I was asking Cara how we could find out which room was Mama's, I saw Emma Lou standing with her sister Bea across the room. They were talking with Austin. She turned and saw me and immediately broke out into a grin as she walked toward me. "CJ, it's so good to see you. My mom told me you were in Truway again." She then looked at Cara and said, "Hi, Cara. I've been wanting to meet you ever since I found out you existed. How do you like Truway?"

"It's a wonderful place. It's nice to meet you too. CJ told me about your famous three-legged race," Cara said.

"Did she tell you that the only reason they won the race is because Bea and I fell in the mud?" Austin asked behind Emma Lou.

"We would have won anyway, Austin. Emma Lou and I had our rhythm down and would have out leaned you at the finish," I said as I smiled up at him.

"Welcome to Chilacothe Farms. Thank you for coming to my birthday party," Austin replied.

"We're glad to be here," Cara said.

"Austin, you have other guests coming in the door. Would you please greet them now? Your cousin is here with her friend from school," Bernice said as she walked up to us and then turned and walked away.

"I'll be back. Please make yourselves at home," Austin said with a sigh.

As soon as he walked away, I heard a loud screeching sound, and I knew there was only one person who sounded like that. It was Sally Jane Nelson. She and Freda Gates were here for Austin's party. I turned to see her showing everyone around her the dress she was wearing. I wonder if it came from Paris.

"Emma Lou, do you happen to know where our mom stayed when she lived here?" Cara asked.

"I know where my mom fed both of you right after you were born because she showed me one time," Emma Lou responded.

After we sang to Austin, Cara, Emma Lou, Bea, and I snuck away and went upstairs. We stopped in front of a closed door down the hall. Emma Lou opened it and said, "This is the room."

We peered inside. "Cara, this is where our mom died," I whispered.

She looked at me with tears in her eyes and then wrapped her arms around my neck and began weeping silently. "CJ, whether Mom died of natural causes or was poisoned, knowing this is the room she died in is more than I can take. It's just so sad."

All of a sudden, we heard someone hiss, "How do you know she died here?

We turned and saw Mrs. Chilacothe standing in the doorway.

Emma Lou was the one who found her voice. "Hello, Mrs. Chilacothe. I thought it would be okay to show the girls around the house. I hope you don't mind."

"I'd rather have everyone downstairs. The party's over, and it's time for everyone to go home." With that being said, she turned and slithered down the stairs. We followed her down, said our good-byes to Austin, Emma Lou, and Bea, and then left.

Aunt Lottie and Aunt Thelma were waiting for us in the car. Neither Cara nor I could bring ourselves to tell them what happened. All we said to her when she asked if we had a good time was, "It was great to see Austin, Emma Lou, and Bea."

Early the next morning, we heard the phone ringing. Aunt Lottie had already left for the day, so I got up to answer it.

"Hello?" I asked.

"Hello, who's talking please?" the voice asked back.

"This is CJ. Who's calling?"

"CJ, this is Geraldine Chilacothe. Is your Aunt Lottie at home?" she asked.

"No, she isn't, Mrs. Chilacothe. May I take a message?" I politely asked.

"Actually, it's you that I want to talk to, CJ. Well, you and Cara, of course."

"Oh, why would you want to talk to us?"

"I heard that you had lunch with Lou Ann Brown. You know she left my employ to go work for your Aunt Lottie. I don't want to assume anything, but I just wanted to let you know that I hold no hard feelings toward Lou Ann for leaving me to work at the salon," she rattled on.

"Mrs. Chilacothe, Lou Ann Brown didn't say anything about why she quit working for you. She did tell us that working for Aunt Lottie is rewarding. Is there something else you need to say?" I snapped.

She kept on as if she didn't hear the tone in my voice, "Would you and Cara be free for lunch today? Bernice and

I'd like to see you both. Austin is here, and I know he'd love to see you."

I started to say no, but I didn't want to pass up an opportunity to see Austin. We faithfully wrote to each other once a week while we were in New Mexico. I also knew this was our chance to question Mrs. Chilacothe and Bernice and watch how they reacted. "Yes, Mrs. Chilacothe. Cara and I'd like to have lunch today. Where would you like for us to meet you?" I asked.

"I want you to come out to the house, of course. We have the best cook in the county, and she will be glad to make anything you'd like."

"How are your cook's chocolate milkshakes?"

"We don't drink many shakes, but I am sure she has time to go to the store and get what she needs to make them."

"Thank you. Is it okay to have tuna salad with the shakes?"

"Chocolate shakes and tuna salad sound delicious. Can you be here at noon on the dot?"

"Noon. Sharp. We'll see you then," I said as I hung up the phone.

"Did I hear you talking with someone on the phone?" Cara rubbed her eyes as she came into the living room.

"Yes, Mrs. Chilacothe called to invite us to lunch with her, Bernice, *and* Austin today at noon." I replied.

"I want to have lunch with Austin but Mrs. Chilacothe and Bernice, not so much," Cara said.

When we arrived at the house, Mrs. Chilacothe was the perfect hostess as she said. "Please come in and sit in the parlor while the cook gets our lunch prepared. I told her to wait until your arrival before making the milkshakes." Bernice was already in the parlor when we walked in, but I didn't see Austin. As if she thought I might ask, Mrs. Chilacothe explained, "Austin had to go into Del Rio on business for his father and won't be able to join us."

Cara turned and looked at me as if to say, *I bet they didn't tell Austin we were invited for lunch today.* I nodded at her to let her know that I agreed.

"Mrs. Chilacothe, it's nice of you to ask us to lunch. I hope you don't mind if we let you eat a few bites first and take a sip of your chocolate shake before we dig in," Cara said as she gave her a brilliant smile.

"It's not polite for the hostess to eat first. Why would you ask me to do such a thing? It's not proper etiquette," she hissed.

"We want you to eat your meals first because we don't want to get sick like Mama did while she was staying here," I interrupted.

"What CJ is trying to say is that we both think it's unfortunate that Mom got sick while staying here. We found out that both of you were giving her something to eat before she died," Cara said.

Bernice turned beet red, but Mrs. Chilacothe's face was ashen as she tried to talk. All of a sudden, she slumped over and fell to the floor. We got up and rushed to see what might have happened. Cara ran to the phone to call 911 just as Austin and his grandfather entered the room.

I didn't know what to say to them. I kept remembering Brother Mike advising us to use our heads. But right now I couldn't think about that. All I could seem to play over and over in my mind was that my mama was poisoned.

The ambulance got to the house quickly. Mr. Chilacothe drove Bernice to the hospital. Austin decided to stay home with us while we waited for Aunt Thelma.

We sat in the parlor in silence, but then Austin started talking to us. "I couldn't sleep last night and got up to get a glass of water. I overheard Mom and Grandmother talking about you two being in town and afraid you would confront them about your mom's death. Grandmother said something about you two having Jean's diary and discovering the truth about your mother's death. Grandmother confessed to Mom that she did put something in her food to cause her to get sick. She was trying to stop the marriage. She believed that Dad would eventually back out of the marriage if he saw how difficult it would be to raise two little girls and have a new wife at the same time.

Then Mom said, "You put poison in Jean's food? I put a drug into her candy to delay the wedding too. All this time, I thought I caused her death, but now I realize you're the one that killed her, not me."

"No, I didn't give her enough poison to kill her. It was supposed to just make her sick. She wasn't supposed to die! If you gave her a drug and I gave her something too, no wonder she died," Grandmother hollered at Mom. He looked at Cara and me with such regret in his eyes.

As it turned out, Mrs. Chilacothe had a stroke and would not be able to talk, use her right arm, or walk until she had therapy, maybe not ever. I know I should care about what happens to her, but right now I cannot bring myself to forget about what we discovered. If I could not ever forget, could I forgive?

I entered into somewhat of a trance for a couple of days. I remember signing papers for the authorities to exhume Mom's body. She died of a heart attack just like Dr. Thompson predicted, but she also had trace amounts of arsenic and another undetectable drug in her system.

We had a small private memorial for Mama in the cemetery. Even though we are with each other every day, Cara and I haven't even taken the time to talk to each other about our feelings. If Sam were here to comfort her, I would feel better about her silence. I thought about going to the church to visit with Brother Mike, but right now, I just want to be by myself. Cara must feel the same way.

Cara finally opened up and shared her feelings with me.

"CJ, I know you are really struggling right now. Even though we predicted something sinister might have happened to Mom, it is difficult to hear the truth and go on with our lives. Please know that I am struggling too and want to bury my head in my pillow for awhile, but I want to be here for you. We have each other, and Mom would want us to go on with our lives."

All I could do was look at Cara and cry. Maybe if we both decided to pray for God to help us with our hurt and anger, he would hear our prayer. Only God could take away our pain.

We heard from Lou Ann Brown that Austin confronted his mom in front of his dad about putting something in Mom's candy. Neither Austin nor his dad could bring themselves to talk to her. With increased guilt and stress and no support at home, she had to go into a mental hospital for awhile.

Cara and I finally returned to church to talk with Brother Mike together. We told him how angry we were for what Mrs. Chilacothe and Bernice did to our mom. We also told him we felt guilty for the outcome of our investigation. We discovered the truth, but it came at a price.

He said, "Girls, I know you are feeling many conflicting emotions right now. You are angry. You feel responsible. However, the choices those ladies made long ago led them to where they are today. The important thing is God asks us to forgive, just as He forgives."

Forgive. Easy to say. Difficult to do.

The sun comes up every morning, and with the promise of a new day comes hope for an even better tomorrow. Aunt Lottie decided to open an additional shop in Truway. She bought the old general store and transformed it into a flower shop. Lou Ann Brown is the manager. CJ and I were her first customers. Not only did we buy flowers for Mom's grave, we bought flowers for Mrs. Chilacothe and sent them to the Del Rio Rehab Center. We also sent flowers to the psychiatric hospital that Bernice was staying in. On both cards, we simply wrote, "God forgives!"

We decided that it would be a nice gesture to send flowers to Mrs. Chilacothe every year on her birthday. Maybe instead of sending them each year, we could make it a point to take flowers to Mama's grave and take a bouquet to Mrs. Chilacothe in person too. It won't be easy, but it's something we need to do. We think Brother Mike would agree.

After a lunch at Della's Diner with Aunt Thelma, Aunt Lottie took us back to the Big Southern Hair.

"CJ, someday this will all be yours and Cara's to run. I hope you will want to keep it in the family. This salon is so much a part of your history," she told us.

"Of course, we'll keep it in the family, Aunt Lottie. I think it would be fun to add a spa at the back. What do you think about that?" I asked.

"Let's wait until spas become more popular. I believe that will happen in your adulthood just as I think big hair is going to make a comeback in the eighties," Aunt Lottie said.

"Here's to the Big Southern Hair and Highlights Beauty Salon!" We toasted with our Cherry Cokes.

"And here's to the comeback of big hair!" Cara toasted.

We all four looked at each other and then started laughing so hard, we were crying.

Epilogue

June 29, 1980

Dear Cara,

I can hardly wait for August to get here because that's when you will be here in person again!

Guess what? Aunt Lottie and I bought Della's Diner. And guess what else? We changed the name to Jean and Joe's Place. I got the idea when I came to help with the Whistle Stop Cafe's fiftieth anniversary two years ago. It's a way to bring a little bit of Daddy to Truway. Don't you know that Mama and Daddy would be so proud to have a place of their own?

You will also be glad to know that I ran into Austin Chilacothe last week, and we had a good talk. Even though the pain is still very much alive, I realize that Austin is not at fault. It was great to see his beautiful smile once again. He plans to take over his grandfather's farm in the fall. He asked if I would have lunch with him sometime, so I told him I would. That was three lunches ago. We sit in the back booth in the café and talk about his plans for the farm and my plans for the three shops we own in town.

Not only will we make our traditional trips to the cemetery and to see Mrs. Chilacothe, we will be celebrating the fiftieth anniversary of the Big Southern Hair! I had a plaque made to put on one of the hair dryers that reads "Big Southern Hair and Highlights, 1930–1980."

It's time to turn in, so I will close for now. It will be wonderful to be with you again. Give Aunt Thelma and Sam a *big* hug from me. You are such a blessing in my life!

Love you forever,
CJ

July 10, 1980

Dear CJ,

It was so good to hear from you! I am excited that our annual get-together is just around the corner. I will be in Truway in exactly a month and look forward to the Big Southern Hair's fiftieth anniversary.

It was good to hear that you and Aunt Lottie bought Della's Diner and changed the name to Jean and Joe's Place! It sounds like you are doing a lot for the economy in Truway. I'm thrilled that you ran into Austin, and that you two are spending worthwhile time together. He has always been a good friend, and no matter what happened in the past or what will happen in the future, he will be someone who has your back.

I have lots of things to share with you. First of all, Glen sends his love. His cardiologist says that his heart is better than he first thought. Glen will need a heart transplant in the future, but he is holding his own until his name comes up on the list. We have decided to spend a few years on the ranch until he gets stronger. Aunt Thelma is so happy that we're here.

You will never guess what we found out. There's going to be a Marfan Syndrome Foundation in Port Washington, New York! Can you believe it? It will be finished early next year, and the founding members have asked Glen and me to attend the ribbon-cutting ceremony!

We are extremely proud to attend. Since we came up with the idea to have a Marfan Syndrome camp at Las Bonitas Ranch each summer, it is only natural to advertise its existence through the foundation. We plan to host the first camp next June. Not only do we want the people with Marfans to visit a week at a time, we want to invite their family members too.

I already painted the sign that I want hung at the front gate. I am sending you a brief sketch of what it looks like. Maybe you can come for the grand opening and see the actual sign. It is only right to put Sam on the sign. After all, he has saved my life more than once, and I want to honor him. He will be a big attraction to the prospective campers.

I don't have any other news at this time. It will be great to see you next month. Until then, give my love to Aunt Lottie. Take care, and know that I thank God for you every day!

Love that never fails,
Cara